P9-DCT-928

At that moment Rhianna became aware of the steady throb of a powerful engine. And she knew, with horror, that they'd sailed.

She almost flung herself at the stateroom door, twisting the handle one way and then another, tugging it, dragging at it breathlessly, refusing to believe that it was actually locked.

Diaz had implied that he was descended from a Spanish pirate, but this was the twenty-first century, for God's sake.

Rhianna faced him, hands folded to hide the fact they were shaking.

"Just what do you think you're doing? Diaz, you're being ridiculous. You can't behave like this."

"And just who is going to stop me?" His voice held faint amusement.

Diaz straightened, coming away from the door and walking across to her. Standing over her so that in spite of herself she shrank back.

"You see, Rhianna, I just don't think you can be trusted. I think you spell trouble in every line of that delectable body." His eyes were hard. "You're coming with me, sweetheart. You might not be my companion of choice, you understand, but— hey—the time will soon pass. We're sailing off into tomorrow's sunrise. Together."

Dear Reader,

Harlequin Presents® is all about passion, power and seduction—along with oodles of wealth and abundant glamour. This is the series of the rich and the superrich. Private jets, luxury cars and international settings that range from the wildly exotic to the bright lights of the big city! We want to whisk you away to the far corners of the globe and allow you to escape to and indulge in a unique world of unforgettable men and passionate romances. There is only one Harlequin Presents. And we promise you the world....

As if this weren't enough, there's more! More of what you love every month. Two weeks after the Presents titles hit the shelves, four Presents EXTRA titles join them! Presents EXTRA is selected especially for you—your favorite authors and much-loved themes have been handpicked to create exclusive collections for your reading pleasure. Now there are more excuses to indulge! Each month, there's a new collection to treasure—you won't want to miss out.

Harlequin Presents—still the original and the best!

Best wishes,

The Editors

Sara Craven

RUTHLESS AWAKENING

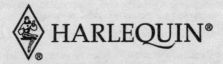

HARLEQUIN®

TORONTO • NEW YORK • LONDON
AMSTERDAM • PARIS • SYDNEY • HAMBURG
STOCKHOLM • ATHENS • TOKYO • MILAN • MADRID
PRAGUE • WARSAW • BUDAPEST • AUCKLAND

If you purchased this book without a cover you should be aware
that this book is stolen property. It was reported as "unsold and
destroyed" to the publisher, and neither the author nor the
publisher has received any payment for this "stripped book."

Recycling programs
for this product may
not exist in your area.

ISBN-13: 978-0-373-12863-1

RUTHLESS AWAKENING

First North American Publication 2009.

Copyright © 2009 by Sara Craven.

All rights reserved. Except for use in any review, the reproduction or
utilization of this work in whole or in part in any form by any electronic,
mechanical or other means, now known or hereafter invented, including
xerography, photocopying and recording, or in any information storage
or retrieval system, is forbidden without the written permission of the
publisher, Harlequin Enterprises Limited, 225 Duncan Mill Road,
Don Mills, Ontario, Canada M3B 3K9.

This is a work of fiction. Names, characters, places and incidents are
either the product of the author's imagination or are used fictitiously,
and any resemblance to actual persons, living or dead, business
establishments, events or locales is entirely coincidental.

This edition published by arrangement with Harlequin Books S.A.

® and TM are trademarks of the publisher. Trademarks indicated with
® are registered in the United States Patent and Trademark Office, the
Canadian Trade Marks Office and in other countries.

www.eHarlequin.com

Printed in U.S.A.

All about the author...
Sara Craven

SARA CRAVEN was born in south Devon, England, and grew up surrounded by books in a house by the sea. After leaving grammar school she worked as a local journalist, covering everything from flower shows to murders. She started writing for Harlequin® Books in 1975. Sara Craven has appeared as a contestant on the U.K. Channel Four game show *Fifteen to One* and in 1997 won the title of Television Mastermind of Great Britain.

Sara shares her Somerset home with several thousand books and an amazing video and DVD collection.

When she's not writing, she likes to travel in Europe, particularly Greece and Italy. She loves music, theater, cooking and eating in good restaurants, but reading will always be her greatest passion.

Since the birth of her twin grandchildren in New York City, she has become a regular visitor to the Big Apple.

CHAPTER ONE

As THE train from London crossed the Tamar, Rhianna felt the butterflies in her stomach turn into sick, churning panic.

I shouldn't be doing this, she thought desperately. I have no right to go to this wedding. To stand in Polkernick Church, watching as Carrie gets married to Simon. I should have kept away. I knew it before the invitation came. And even before it was made forcefully clear to me that I wouldn't be welcome. That I should keep my distance.

So how can I be on this train—making this journey?

Ever since the engagement had been announced she'd been dreading the arrival of the elegantly embossed card, and had already drafted her polite letter of regret with the same excuse— the shooting schedule on the next series—that she'd previously used to get out of being a bridesmaid.

And then Carrie had phoned unexpectedly to say she was coming to London trousseau-shopping, and would Rhianna meet her for a girls' lunch?

'You must come, darling.' Her voice had been eager, laughing. 'Because it might just be the last one now that Simon's got this job in Cape Town. Heaven knows when we'll be back in the UK.'

'Cape Town?' Rhianna had heard the sharp note in her voice and cursed herself. She'd made herself speak more lightly. 'I had no idea that he—that you were planning to live abroad.' *Nothing's been said...*

'Oh, it wasn't planned,' Carrie had said blithely. 'Someone Diaz knows had an opening in his company, and made Simon an offer that was too good to miss.'

Diaz...

Rhianna had repeated the name under her breath, tension clenching like a fist in her stomach. Yes, she'd thought dully. Painfully. It would have to be Diaz. Making sure that Simon was removed to a safe distance. Out of harm's way. Regardless of the damage already done, which would be left behind.

Diaz—twitching the strings from across continents and oceans to make sure the puppets danced to his tune, and that Carrie, his much-loved young cousin, would walk up the aisle of the twelfth-century church in the village to be united with the man she'd adored since childhood.

The perfect match, she'd thought, her throat tightening. And nothing would be allowed to prevent it.

She should have made some excuse about lunch, and she knew it, but she'd been torn between the pleasure of seeing Carrie again and the anguish of keeping silent while the other girl talked about Simon and her plans for the wedding. Of making sure that not one word, one look or one hint escaped her.

But, dear God, it had been so hard to sit opposite Carrie and see her pretty face radiant with happiness. To see the dream in her eyes and know how hideously simple it would be to turn that inner vision into a nightmare.

How simple, and how utterly impossible.

'So you will be coming to the wedding—you promise faithfully?' Carrie had begged. 'You'll introduce a note of sanity into the proceedings, darling. A rock for me to cling to, because by then I'll need it,' she'd added, shuddering. 'With the respective mothers already circling each other in a state of armed neutrality. I reckon there could be blood on the carpet before the great day dawns.'

And Rhianna had agreed. Because the only reasons she was left with to justify her absence were the ones she could never say.

But mainly because Carrie was her friend. Had been her first real friend, and shown her the only genuine kindness she'd ever known at Penvarnon. She—and Simon, of course. Which was how the trouble had first begun...

And now Carrie, who loved her, was here to make innocently sure that wild horses wouldn't keep Rhianna from attending her wedding.

But wild horses didn't even feature, Rhianna thought, her mouth twisting harshly. Not when they were up against the arrogant power of Diaz Penvarnon.

Against whose expressed will she was travelling to Cornwall. Defying his mandate.

His anger had been like a dark cloud, waiting in the corner of her mind to become a storm. A tangible thing, as if he were still standing over her, his lean face inimical.

'Don't say you weren't warned...'

As she remembered, her mouth felt suddenly dry, and she uncapped the bottle of mineral water on the table in front of her and drank it down without bothering with the glass the attendant had brought her.

Pull yourself together, she thought. You'll be in Cornwall for three days—four at the outside. And once Carrie's wedding is over you'll be gone—for good this time.

Besides, Diaz probably won't even be there. He'll be back in South America, arrogantly confident that his commands will be obeyed in his absence.

The rest of the occupants of that big grey stone house on the headland might not relish her presence, but there was no one who could really hurt her any more, she thought, her mouth tightening. No one to look down on her or treat her like an intruder. That section of her life was in the past, and she would make sure it stayed that way.

Because she was no longer the housekeeper's unwanted niece, the skinny waif that the daughter of the house, Caroline Seymour, had inexplicably and unsuitably decided to befriend and had stubbornly refused to give up in the face of concerted family opposition.

She was Rhianna Carlow, television actress and current star of the award winning drama series *Castle Pride*. An independent woman, with her own life and her own flat, who didn't have to dress in clothing from charity shops and jumble sales any more, or say thank you to anyone but herself.

She was a success—a face that people recognised. A few hours ago she'd seen some of the other passengers in this first-class carriage nudging each other and whispering as she'd taken her seat at Paddington.

She knew from past experience that it would only be a matter of time before someone asked her for an autograph, or permission to take a picture of her with a mobile phone, because that was generally what happened. And she would smile and acquiesce, so that the person asking the favour would go away saying how lovely she was—how charming.

And another brief performance would have been given.

But that was the easy part of being Rhianna Carlow. Because she knew it would take every scrap of acting ability she possessed to stand in silence the day after tomorrow and watch Carrie become Simon's wife. To hear him say, 'Forsaking all others...' when he knew that she, Rhianna, would be in the congregation, listening to him, angry, hurt—and above all, anxious for Carrie.

When every nerve in her body would be urging her to cry out, No, this can't happen. I won't let it. It has to stop right here—right now. For everyone's sake.

And weren't you supposed to be cruel in order to be kind? she asked herself restlessly. Wasn't that one of the relentless clichés that people trotted out, usually to justify some piece of deliberate malice?

But could she stand up and tell the truth and see the light slowly die from Carrie's bright face when she realised just how fundamentally Simon had betrayed her?

It would be like, she thought dispassionately, watching an eclipse of the sun, knowing that this time it would be permanent and there would be no returning radiance.

Carrie had always been a sunshine girl, lit from within, fair-haired and merry-faced, drawing Rhianna, the outsider, the dark moon, into her orbit.

Compensating over and over again for her aunt Kezia's unrelenting coldness, and the aloofness bordering on hostility displayed by the rest of the family at Penvarnon House.

From the first day that was how it had been, she thought. When she'd stood, an unhappy twelve-year-old, shivering in the brisk wind, at the top of the flight of steps that led down to the lawns, knowing guiltily that already she'd broken her aunt's first rule that she should never—ever—stray into the environs of the house and its grounds.

Knowing that her home was now a chillingly neat flat, converted from the former stable block, and that if she wished to play she should do so only in the stable yard outside.

'Allowing you here is a great concession by Mrs Seymour, and you must always be grateful for that,' Aunt Kezia had told her repressively. 'But it's on condition that you confine your activities to our own quarters and not go beyond them. Do you understand?'

No, Rhianna had thought with a kind of desolate rebellion, I don't understand. I don't know why Mummy had to die, or why I couldn't stay in London with Mr and Mrs Jessop, because they offered to have me. I don't know why you came and brought me away to a place where no one wants me—least of all you. A place with the sea all round it, cutting me off from everything I know. Somewhere that I don't want to be.

She hadn't meant to be disobedient, but the minimal attractions of the stable yard, with its cobbles and long-unused row of loose boxes, had palled within minutes, and a half-open gate had beckoned to her in a way it had been impossible to resist. Just a quick look, she'd promised herself, at the place where she'd be spending the next few years of her life, then she would come back, and close the gate, and no-one would be any the wiser.

So, she'd followed the gravel walk round the side of the looming bulk that was Penvarnon House and found herself at its rear, confronted by lawns that stretched to the very edge of the headland. And racing across the grass towards her had been two children.

The girl had reached the foot of the steps first, and looked up, laughing.

'Hello. I'm Carrie Seymour, and this is Simon. Has your mother brought you to have tea? How grim and grizzly. We were just going down to the cove, so why don't you come with us instead?'

'I can't.' Rhianna swallowed, dismally realising the trouble she was in.

'I shouldn't even be here. My aunt told me I must stay by the stables.'

'Your aunt?' the girl asked, and paused. 'Oh, you must be Miss Trewint's niece,' she went on more slowly, adding doubtfully, 'I heard Mummy and Daddy talking about you.' There was another silence, then her face brightened again. 'But you can't hang round the yard all day with nothing to do. That's silly. Come with Simon and me. I'll make it all right with Mother and Miss Trewint, you'll see.'

And somehow, miraculously, she had done exactly that—by dint, Rhianna thought drily, of smiling seraphically and refusing to budge. Just like always.

Rhianna, she'd insisted cheerfully, had come to live at Penvarnon House and therefore they would be friends. End of story.

And start of another, very different narrative, Rhianna thought. Although none of us knew it at the time. A story of past secrets, unhappiness and betrayal. And this time there would be no happy ending.

I should have stayed by the stables, she thought with irony. It was safer there. I should never have gone down the path to the cove and spent the afternoon climbing over rocks, peering into pools, running races along the sand and splashing barefoot in the freezing shallows of the sea. Discovering childhood again. Drawing my first breath of happiness in weeks.

She'd assumed that Simon—tall, also blond-haired and blue-eyed, and clearly older than Carrie by a couple of years or more—was Carrie's brother, but she had been mistaken.

'My brother? Heavens, no. Both of us are "onlys", like you,' Carrie had said blithely. 'He's just a grockle—an emmet.' And she'd dodged, laughing, as Simon lunged at her with a menacing growl.

'What's a—grockle?' Rhianna asked doubtfully.

'An incomer,' Simon informed her, pulling a face. 'A tourist. Someone who doesn't live in Cornwall but only comes here for holidays. And an emmet is an ant,' he added, looking darkly at Carrie. 'Because in the summer that's what the tourists are like—all over the place in droves. But we're not either of those things, because we have a house just outside the village and spend half our lives down here.'

'So we have to put up with him for weeks at a time,' Carrie said mournfully. 'What an utter drag.'

But even then, young as they all were, some instinct had told Rhianna that Carrie didn't mean it, and that Simon, the golden, the glorious, was already the centre of her small universe.

Both of them, she'd discovered, would be going back to their respective boarding schools at the end of the Easter holidays, whereas she would be attending the local secondary school at Lanzion.

'But there'll be half-term to look forward to,' Carrie had said eagerly. 'And then we'll have nearly eight weeks in the summer. The sea's really safe down at the cove, so we can swim every day, and have picnics, and if the weather's foul we can use The Cabin.'

She was referring to the large wooden building tucked under the cliff, which, as Rhianna was to discover, not only housed sunbeds and deckchairs, but had a spacious living area with its own tiny galley kitchen, an ancient sagging sofa, and a table big enough to sit round to eat or play games. The late Ben Penarvon, Diaz's father, had even had the place wired for electricity.

'It's going to be great,' Carrie had added, her grin lighting up the world. 'I'm really glad you came to live here.'

And even Aunt Kezia's overt disapproval, and the fact that Moira Seymour, Carrie's mother, had looked right through her on their rare encounters, had not been able to take the edge off Rhianna's growing contentment. The feeling that she could relax and allow herself to feel more settled.

She'd still grieved for her mother—the more so since Aunt Kezia had made it clear that any mention of Grace Carlow's name was taboo. At the same time Rhianna had realised that there was not one photograph of her mother, or any family mementoes, anywhere in the cheerless little flat. Moreover, her own framed photo of her parents' wedding, which she'd put on the table beside her narrow bed, had been removed and placed in the chest of drawers.

'I have quite enough to do in the house,' Aunt Kezia had returned brusquely when Rhianna, upset, had tried to protest. 'I'm not coming back here and having to dust round your nonsense.'

On the upside, she'd liked her new school, too, and had come home at the end of the summer term excited at being given a part in the school play, which would be rehearsed during the autumn and staged before Christmas.

But, to her shock and disappointment, Aunt Kezia had rounded on her. 'You'll do nothing of the kind,' she declared tight-lipped. 'I won't have you putting yourself forward, giving yourself airs, because it only leads to trouble. And there's been too much of that in the past,' she added with angry bitterness. 'Quite apart from this nonsense with Miss Caroline. And after all I said to you, too.'

She drew a harsh breath. 'Kindly remember that you're only here on sufferance, my girl, and learn to keep in the background more than you have been doing while you're living in Mrs Seymour's house.'

'But it isn't her house,' Rhianna objected. 'Carrie told me it really belongs to her cousin, Diaz, but he's away most of the time, either living on his other estates in South America or travelling all over the world as a mining consultant. So her parents look after it for him. She says when he decides to get married they'll have to find somewhere else to live.'

'Miss Caroline says a deal too much,' her aunt said grimly. 'And I'm still going to have a word with your teacher. Knock this acting nonsense on the head once and for all.'

And, in spite of Rhianna's tearful protests, she'd done exactly that.

'Poor you,' Carrie had said, her forehead wrinkled with concern when Rhianna had eventually told her what had happened. 'She's so hard on you all the time. Has she always been like that?'

Rhianna shook her head. 'I don't know,' she said unhappily. 'I only met her for the first time when she came to Mummy's funeral and told me that she'd been appointed my legal guardian and I had to live with her. Before that I'd never heard from her at all—not even on my birthday or at Christmas. And I could tell she was angry about having to take me.' She sighed. 'I'm not really welcome here either. I just wish someone would tell me what I've done that's so wrong.'

'It's not you,' Carrie said hesitantly. 'I—I'm sure it's not.'

Rhianna bit her lip. 'You said once you'd heard your parents talking about me. Would you tell me what they said?'

Carrie's face was pink with dismay. After a pause, she said, 'It was ages ago, so I'm not sure I remember exactly. Besides, I shouldn't have been listening anyway,' she added glumly. 'And I'm sure it would be better coming from your aunt.'

'She won't talk about it,' Rhianna said bitterly. 'She doesn't talk about anything.' She looked beseechingly at the other girl. 'Oh, please, Carrie. I really need to know why they all seem to hate me so much.'

Carrie sighed. 'Well—I was on the window seat in the drawing room, reading, and my parents came in. They didn't realise I was there, and Mummy was saying, "I can hardly believe that Kezia Trewint would do such a thing. Agree to take in that woman's child—and have the gall to ask to bring her here." Daddy said he supposed she hadn't had much choice in the matter, and he told Mummy not to do anything too hasty, because they'd never find anyone to run the house and cook as well as your aunt.'

She swallowed. 'Then he said, "And it's hardly the child's fault. You can't blame her for things that her mother did years before she was born. And that's how it was, so don't start thinking anything nonsensical." Then Mummy got cross and said that your mother was—not a nice person,' Carrie added in a little embarrassed rush. 'And that the apple never fell far from the tree, and what the hell would Diaz say when he heard? Daddy said, "God only knows," and he thought that everyone should reserve judgement and give you a chance. Then he went off to the golf club.'

She added tearfully, 'I'm so sorry, Rhianna. I should never have listened, but when I met you I was really glad, because you looked so unhappy and lost, and I told myself that Daddy was right. Only now I'm afraid I've made everything a hundred times worse.'

'No,' Rhianna said slowly. 'No, you haven't—I promise. Because I—I really wanted to know.' She flung back her head. 'Besides, none of it's true. Mummy wasn't a bit like that. She was a wonderful person.'

And so beautiful too, she thought, with all that deep, dark auburn hair that Daddy said was the colour of mahogany, and the green eyes that tilted at the corners when she laughed. Whereas my hair is just—red.

She swallowed. 'After Daddy died she got a job as a care worker, and the people she visited really loved her. They all said so. And Mrs Jessop told someone that if Mummy hadn't been so involved with looking after everyone else she might have thought about herself more, and realised there was something wrong. Seen a doctor before it was—too late.' Her voice wobbled. 'So, you see, there must be some mistake. There *has* to be.'

Carrie gave her a comforting pat. 'I'm sure,' she said, but her anxious eyes said that even if her parents had been wrong, that still didn't explain Kezia Trewint's strange, unloving attitude to her only living relative.

Understanding that had still been a long way in the future, Rhianna thought wearily, leaning back in her seat and closing her eyes. In the meantime it had remained on the edge of her life, a cloud no bigger than a man's hand, yet occasionally ominously hinting at the storm to come.

Like the day she'd encountered Diaz Penvarnon for the first time.

It had been, she remembered, one of those burning, windless days in August, when the sun seemed close enough to touch.

They'd been down at the beach all day, slipping in and out of the unruffled sea like seals, Rhianna by then as competent and confident a swimmer as the other two. It had been Simon who'd called a halt, explaining that he needed to get back as his parents had friends coming to dinner.

In spite of the heat, it had always been a matter of honour to see who could get to the top of the cliff path ahead of the others. The girls rarely won against Simon's long legs, but this particu-

lar afternoon he had dropped one of his new trainers in the loose
sand at the foot of the cliff and halted to retrieve it, so that Carrie
and Rhianna had found themselves unexpectedly ahead, flying
neck and neck up the stony track.

And when Carrie had stumbled Rhianna had got there first,
laughing and breathless, head down as she launched herself
towards some invisible finishing tape.

Only to cannon into something tall, solid and all too real,
finding, as she had staggered back with a gasp of shock, strong
hands grasping her shoulders to steady her, while a man's cool
voice had said, 'So—what have we here? A fleeing trespasser?
This is private land, you know.'

She looked up dazedly into the face above her, swarthy and
lean, with high cheekbones only to see the faint amusement fade
from the firm mouth and the grey eyes become as icy as snow
clouds in January. He studied her in return, his glance shifting
with a kind of incredulity from her unruly cloud of hair to her
long-lashed eyes and her startled, parted lips.

She said, 'I'm Rhianna Carlow. I—I live here.'

He drew a swift sharp breath, lifting his hands from her and
stepping back in a repudiation that was as instant as it was unmistakable.

He said, half to himself, 'Of course—the child. I'd almost
forgotten.'

'Diaz!' Carrie was there, hurling herself at him. 'How truly
great! No one said you were coming.'

'It was intended as a surprise,' he said, returning her exuber-
ant hug with more restraint before he looked back at Rhianna.
He added unsmilingly, 'It seems to be a day for them.'

And she thought with inexplicable desolation, Someone else
who doesn't want me to be here…

Simon's panting arrival provided a momentary diversion,
but the greetings were barely over before Moira Seymour
came sauntering across the lawn towards them, cool in a blue
cotton dress, and fanning herself languidly with a broad-
brimmed straw hat.

She said, 'Simon, my pet, your mother's telephoned, asking

where you are. Carrie, darling, get cleaned up for tea, please.'
Her glance flickered dismissively over Rhianna. 'And I'm sure,
young woman, that your aunt can find something for you to do.'

The first direct remark Mrs Seymour had ever made to her,
Rhianna realised. And one that made her inferior position in the
household quite explicit. Turning her back into the intruder. The
trespasser that Diaz Penvarnon had just called her. A name that
might have started as a joke, but was now, suddenly, something
very different.

My first starring role, Rhianna thought bitterly, and one that
will probably haunt me, for so many reasons, as long as I live,
wherever I go, and whatever happens to me.

Diaz—Diaz Penvarnon...

He was a chain, she told herself, linking her with the past,
which must be broken now that he was out of her life for ever.

I've got to start thinking of him as a stranger, she thought,
almost feverishly. I must...

But from that first moment of meeting he'd imprinted himself
indelibly on her consciousness, and Rhianna had found her life
changing once more—and not for the better, either.

Because she had once more been strictly relegated to the flat
over the stables and its immediate vicinity, pretty much reduced
to the status of non-person again, while a protesting Carrie had
simply been whipped away and absorbed into the sudden surge
of activities at the house itself, putting her out of reach for the
duration of the owner's visit.

The owner...

Even at a distance, Rhianna had sensed that the whole place
seemed to have lost its languid, almost melancholy atmosphere
and become—re-energised.

And that had been even without the constant stream of visitors
filling the place at weekends, flocking down to the cove to swim
and sunbathe, or play tennis on the newly marked court at the
side of the house. Not forgetting the dinner parties that went on
into the early hours, with music spilling out through the open
windows into the warm nights, and dancers moving on the terrace.

With Diaz Penarvon at the forefront of it all.

On the few occasions that Rhianna had dared venture further than the stable yard she had seen that. Had recognised that his tall figure seemed to be everywhere, exercising effortless dominion over his surroundings, as if he'd never been absent, with the cool, incisive voice she'd remembered only too well issuing orders that were immediately obeyed.

'And I wonder how Madam likes that?' Rhianna had overheard Mrs Welling, the daily help, comment with a chuckle to Jacky Besant, who worked in the grounds, while they were enjoying a quiet smoke in the yard.

'Not much, I reckon.' Jacky had also seemed amused. 'But she's no need to fret. He'll be gone again soon enough, and then she'll have it easy again.'

Maybe we all will, Rhianna had thought, stifling a sigh.

It had occurred to her that Diaz wasn't a bit as she'd imagined when Carrie had first told her about him.

For one thing she'd assumed he'd be much older. Physically much heavier, too. Not lean, rangy, and possessed of a dynamism she'd been able to recognise even at her immature age.

'He's what they call a babe magnet,' Simon, himself sidelined under the new regime, had commented resentfully when Rhianna, sent on an errand by her aunt, had met him emerging from the village Post Office. 'Tall, dark and mega-rich. My parents say that every female in Cornwall under thirty is trying to have a crack at him.'

'Well, I think he's vile,' Rhianna said vehemently, remembering how those extraordinary eyes—almost silver under their dark fringe of lashes—had frozen her.

Recalling too how she'd seen him in a corner of the terrace one evening, when she'd slipped round to listen to the music. How she'd become aware of a movement in the shadows and realised he was there, entwined with some blonde girl in a way that had made her burn with embarrassment, together with other sensations less easy to define.

And how, as he'd pushed the dress from his companion's shoulders, she'd turned and run back to her own domain, and not ventured out at night again.

Now, she added with renewed emphasis, 'Sick-making.'

Simon grinned faintly. 'Keep thinking that way.' He paused. 'Fancy going down to the harbour for an ice cream or a Coke at Rollo's Café?'

She shook her head. 'I—I have to get back.' It was only partly true. She didn't want to admit that she'd been sent out with the exact money to pay for her aunt's requirements and no more.

'You can be spared for ten minutes, surely?' Simon said reasonably. 'And you need something cool before you bike back to Penvarnon or you'll be roasted.' He paused. 'My treat.'

She flushed with pleasure. Simon the cool and totally gorgeous was actually offering to buy her an ice cream. Normally he didn't take a great deal of notice of her, when Carrie was there. They'd been friends long before she came on the scene, and she'd always accepted that, told herself it was nasty of her to feel even slightly envious.

But now Carrie was occupied, and she had this one blissful chance to spend a little while with Simon on her own. Without, she thought, having to share him. And instantly felt thoroughly ashamed of herself.

Then she saw Simon smiling at her, and drew a small, happy breath. 'I mustn't be too long,' she temporised.

He bought their ice creams, and they sat on the harbour wall in the sunshine, watching the boats and chatting about everything and nothing, until Rhianna said regretfully she really had to get back, and Simon lifted her down from the rough stones.

'Hey,' he said. 'This has been great. We must do it again.'

As she'd cycled back to Penvarnon her heart had been singing. It might only been half an hour, but for Rhianna it had become thirty minutes framed in gold. A pivotal moment for a lonely girl on the verge of adolescence. Heady stuff.

But certainly not enough to provide the foundation for any dreams about the future.

But I didn't know that then, she thought unhappily. And it was long, long in the future before I realised that by the time you're sure of your dream and want it to come true it may be completely beyond your reach.

She was startled out of her reverie by the train manager's voice announcing the express's imminent arrival at her station.

Rhianna rose, reaching for her sunglasses, reluctantly collecting her suitcase and dress carrier as she prepared to alight.

You don't have to do this, an inner voice urged. You could stay right here, extend your ticket to Penzance, and from there catch the next train back to London. Then make the excuse you've been hit by some virus. Summer flu. Anything…

Carrie will be disappointed if you don't show, but that will surely be a minor issue when she has so much else to be happy about.

And if you can't stand the idea of London, then get yourself to the nearest airport. You've got your passport in your bag, plus your credit cards, so buy a flight somewhere—anywhere—and chill out for a while.

And stop—stop agonising over the past. Because there's nothing you can do—not without ruining Carrie's happiness. And that's never been an option.

But she was already caught up in the small stream of people who were also leaving the train. The door in front of her had opened, and she was stepping down into the sunlight.

It was hot, but Rhianna felt the fine hairs on her arms react as if a chill wind had touched them.

She paused, all her senses suddenly alert, and saw him.

He was waiting at the back of the platform, taller and darker than anyone else in the bustling crowd around them. A shadow in the sun. His anger like a raised fist. Waiting for her, as she'd somehow known he would be. As she'd felt him deep in her heart—her bones—even while she was trying to convince herself that he'd be long gone, a thousand miles away, and that she had nothing more to fear.

Then, as their eyes met, Diaz Penvarnon began to walk towards her.

CHAPTER TWO

RETREAT was impossible, of course. There were people behind her, and she was being carried forward by their momentum. Towards him.

And then a voice beside her said, 'It's Rhianna Carlow, isn't it? Lady Ariadne from *Castle Pride*. This is a bit of luck. May I have a quick word?'

Rhianna turned quickly to the newcomer, youngish and thin-faced, his brown hair slicked back, his smile confident, but her relief was short-lived.

'I'm Jason Tully,' he went on. 'From the *Duchy Herald*. May I ask what you're doing so far from London? They're not planning to shift the new *Castle Pride* series down to Cornwall, are they?'

'Not as far as I know.' She could handle this, she thought, making herself smile back, every nerve in her body tinglingly aware that Diaz Penvarnon was standing only a couple of feet away. 'Although that would be lovely, of course. *But* I'm actually here on a private visit.'

She was careful not to mention it was a wedding, in case her presence there was enough for him to rouse the rest of the press pack and bring them homing in on Polkernick Church.

Which would no doubt be interpreted as her deliberate attempt to upstage the bride, she thought bitterly.

'I see.' He signalled to an older stouter man, carrying a camera, then looked past her to the train. 'So, are you travelling alone, Rhianna? You don't have a companion?'

'I'm on my way to see friends,' she returned, not daring to look at Diaz and see his reaction.

'Sure.' Jason Tully grinned again. 'I guess you know it's just been announced that your co-star Rob Winters has split up with his wife? I'm wondering how you feel about that?'

Ah, so that's who you were expecting to see following me off the train, you little weasel.

She suppressed an inward groan.

'No, I hadn't heard that,' she returned steadily, aware that Diaz was absorbing every word of the exchange, brows lifted cynically, that other people were halting to stare—and listen. 'And if it's true I'm—sorry. However, I'm certain that it's a temporary difficulty which will soon be resolved.'

'But you and Rob Winters are pretty close?' he persisted. 'Those were some very torrid love scenes you played in the last series.'

'Yes,' Rhianna said. 'We *played* them. Because we're actors, Mr Tully, and that's what we're paid for.'

And you will never know, she thought, how true that is—for me, anyway.

She added, 'And now—if there's nothing else...?'

'Just a picture, if you don't mind.' He looked at Diaz, standing in silence, his hands on his jean-clad hips. 'And you are?'

'Miss Carlow's driver.' Diaz stepped forward and took the bags from her unresisting hands. All of them, she realised too late, including her handbag, with her money, return ticket and everything else.

'I'll be waiting in the car—madam,' he added, as he turned away, heading for the exit. Leaving her staring after him.

'We only came down here to do a story about the delay in track repairs,' Jason Tully announced jubilantly as Rhianna recovered herself, posing obediently for the camera. 'This is a real bonus.'

Your bonus, she thought. But my can of worms.

'Have a nice visit,' he added as she began to walk away. 'I hope you enjoy yourself with your—friends. When you meet up with them.'

The innuendo was unmistakable, and she rewarded it with

another dazzling smile, wishing that she could knock him down and jump on him.

He'll be on to the nationals as soon as he can get his mobile phone out of his pocket, she thought bitterly as she left the station. I only hope that idiot Rob is staying with his parents in Norfolk, and hasn't chosen to go to ground somewhere, in true dramatic fashion. Or nowhere west of Bristol, anyway.

But she couldn't worry about that now. She had her own problems to deal with. The most major of which was standing beside his Jeep, his face bleak and hostile, his pale eyes brooding as he watched her walk towards him.

Her mouth felt dry, and her hands were clammy. If there had been anywhere to go she'd have turned and run. But that wasn't possible, so she'd have to fall back on sheer technique.

Treat it as stage fright, she thought. Then go on and give a performance. The kind that saves the show.

'Mr Penvarnon,' she said, her voice cool and detached. 'What a surprise. I thought you'd be on the other side of the world.'

'You hoped,' he said, as he opened the passenger door for her. 'Was that why you decided to ignore my advice?

Her brows lifted. 'Is that what it was?' she asked ironically. She climbed into the vehicle, making a business of smoothing the skirt of her plain *café au lait* linen dress over her knees. 'I thought I was being threatened. And I don't respond well to threats.'

'But you deal very well with inconvenient questions from reporters, I notice,' Diaz said smoothly. 'I'm so glad you didn't use that coy old cliché, We're just good friends, when he was quizzing you about your involvement with Robert Winters.' He paused. 'So, what is he? Your consolation prize for missing out on the man you love?'

Her heart seemed to stop, but she managed to keep her voice level.

'No,' she said. 'Both Rob and his wife are genuinely friends of mine, but Daisy and I are closer because we met at drama school. And the reason they're having problems is that she wants to stop work and have a baby, whereas he sees them as some starry theatrical couple on a smooth and uninterrupted ride to the top. I see no reason to mention that to the press, local or national.'

She paused, drawing a swift breath that she tried to keep steady. 'And I'm telling you this only because I'm sick of the implication that any other woman's man is fair game as far as I'm concerned.'

'Your protest is touching,' he said, as the Jeep moved forward. 'But the evidence is against you.' His mouth twisted. 'Perhaps it's genetic.'

'If you mean like mother, like daughter,' she said. 'Why don't you just say so? I have no objection. Because I know that whatever my mother did it was for love, and that I *am* no different.'

'Slow curtain,' he said sardonically, 'and tumultuous applause. I loved the authentic quiver of sincerity in the voice, sweetheart. You could make a living in straight drama without needing to take your clothes off on television. But perhaps you enjoy it.'

He paused. 'Incidentally, how did this *good friend* of yours react to the sight of you cavorting naked with her husband?'

She shrugged. 'She thought it was funny.'

Even now she could remember being in Daisy's kitchen, the pair of them hooting with uncontrollable laughter as they waited for Rob to come back with their Indian takeaway.

'Do you know how long it took me,' Daisy had asked tearfully, 'to put concealer on his bum because he thought he was getting a spot?'

'He didn't mention that.' Rhianna shook her head, hiccupping. 'He just kept c-complaining about the draught on the set.'

'He does that when we're in bed,' said his loving wife, wiping her eyes. 'Invariably at the wrong moment. He's terrified of catching a cold. Some people have champagne in their fridges. We have gargle, bless him.'

God, but they were so right for each other, Rhianna thought. Rob—his ambition and talent battling his anxieties. Daisy— serenely grounded.

Their love for each other had been unquestioned and unquestioning—until Daisy's biological clock began ticking away.

If they *were* now separated it had to be a glitch, she told herself passionately, because they belonged together in a way she could only observe and admire. And, if she was honest, envy.

'So what are you doing here, Rhianna?' Diaz's voice broke harshly across her thoughts. His hands were gripping the wheel so fiercely that the knuckles stood out. 'God knows there isn't a soul that wants you at Penvarnon—apart, I suppose, from Carrie. In her case, love is indeed blind, or she'd have seen you a long time ago for the treacherous, self-serving little madam you really are.'

'Heavens,' she said. 'What a turn of phrase. If we ever need a scriptwriter for *Castle Pride* I'll recommend you. Unless, of course, you're planning an alternative career as a cabbie?'

'You didn't really think I'd risk Simon coming to meet you from the train?' he said softly. 'Because my poor trusting Carrie would have let him do it if I hadn't stepped in.'

'Dear me,' she said lightly. 'Is he so little to be relied upon?'

'No.' His voice hardened. 'You are. You're the loose cannon around here. The snake in the grass. And don't think I'll let that slip my mind even for a minute.'

They were outside the town by now, and he swung the wheel suddenly and sharply, pulling the Jeep on to the verge at the side of the road and bringing it to an abrupt halt.

'And this isn't more advice,' he went on. 'It's a warning to be taken seriously.'

He drew a deep breath. 'You probably have every red-blooded man in Britain lusting after you, but that's not enough for you— is it? Because you didn't learn your lesson five years ago. You had to make another play for Simon, and this time it worked.'

He paused. 'But, sadly for you, the Rhianna effect didn't last. You can't have been too pleased when the stupid bastard came to his senses just in time, and realised what was genuine and worthwhile in his life, and how easily he could have lost it. After all you're irresistible—according to the television company's publicity machine.'

His voice roughened. 'You betrayed the best, most loyal friend you've ever had in order to bed Simon, just to prove that you could. But on Saturday she's still the one he's going to marry. And you will say nothing and do nothing to jeopardise that in any way. Do I make myself clear?'

'As crystal.' She stared straight ahead of her through the wind-screen. 'Tell me—did Simon receive a similar lecture, or was this fascinating diatribe designed for me alone?'

'I didn't need to have another go at him,' he said. 'Simon is subdued enough already. And he's made it clear that he bitterly regrets the criminal stupidity of putting his entire future on the line, however potent the temptation. I recommend you keep out of his way,' he added grimly.

'No problem,' she said. 'It's not as if we'll be sharing a roof for the next two nights, after all. And if you're concerned about the daylight hours, why not ask the Hendersons if they'll move out of the flat and put me back in the stables—the servants' quarters—where I belong?'

'When,' he said harshly, 'did you ever *belong* anywhere at Penvarnon?'

She should have expected it, but for a moment Rhianna felt her throat close in shock.

But I never wanted to be there. She wanted to say it aloud. Shout it. *Not once. And I left as soon as I could. If it wasn't for Carrie, I wouldn't be here now. And once these next few ghastly days are behind us, you'll never—ever—see me again.*

But she remained silent. Because he would no more believe her now than he'd done in the past, so there was no point in hoping.

She simply had to deal with the present pain, and face the uncertainty of the future. Both of which she would accomplish alone.

Then his hand moved. The engine roared into life and the Jeep moved forward.

Taking them to Penvarnon.

'Alone at last.' Carrie's laughter had an edge to it, and her hug was fierce. 'Oh, Rhianna, I'm so thankful that you're here. Wasn't it ghastly downstairs just now? You must have noticed.'

'You could have cut the atmosphere with a knife,' Rhianna conceded drily as she returned the hug. 'But I attributed that to my arrival.'

'Don't you believe it,' Carrie returned. 'Besides, no one cares about a lot of old nonsense that happened years ago. Not any more.'

Don't they? Oh, God, don't they? What makes you so sure? Because I can think of one person at least who hasn't forgotten a thing. Or forgiven...

She was still shaking inside, she thought, as she had been throughout the remainder of that taut, silent drive to the house. Seated beside him, hands clamped in her lap. Staring at nothing.

Still shaking when she reached for the door handle almost before the car had stopped on the wide sweep in front of the main entrance and swung herself recklessly, desperately, out on to the gravel.

She'd thought—imagined—just for a moment that Diaz had very quietly said her name, and in that instant had been tempted to turn and look at him.

Only to see Carrie, almost dancing with excitement at the top of the shallow stone steps, while Henderson, very correct in dark trousers and a linen jacket, came down to collect her luggage. So she'd walked towards the house instead.

And as they'd moved inside she'd heard the car drive off—fast.

Swallowing, she now applied herself to the task in hand— hanging the dress carrier in the elegant wardrobe and unzipping her travel bag. 'So, what's the problem?'

Carrie sighed. 'Just that the bell seems to have gone for round fifty in the battle of the mothers. Dad says it's like Waterloo— "a damned close-run thing"—then disappears to the golf club. His answer to everything these days,' she added, with an unwonted hint of bitterness.

'Well, you can't expect him to take a passionate interest in hemlines, flower arrangements and tiers on the cake.' Rhianna tried to sound soothing. 'He probably thinks it's his duty just to keep quiet and write the cheques. Besides,' she added, 'knowing that he's going to have to give you away very soon now and watch you disappear to Cape Town must be preying on his mind, too. Maybe he needs time and space to deal with that?'

'It's going to be hard for me too,' Carrie admitted unhappily. 'Oh, Rhianna, Simon and I—we are doing the right thing, aren't we?'

Rhianna's heart lurched. 'In what way?' She tried to sound casual.

'The new job. I sometimes get the feeling that Simon's having second thoughts about it. He's been so quiet over the past few weeks. Yet when I ask him he says everything's fine.'

Rhianna bent over her case, letting a swathe of waving mahogany hair hide her sudden flush. 'Then probably everything is,' she said constrictedly. 'And don't forget that it's only a job, Carrie, not a life sentence. If it doesn't work out, you move on.'

'I suppose so. But Diaz probably wouldn't be too pleased about that.'

'And is the maintenance of his goodwill really so vital?' She tried to speak lightly. 'Or just a habit?'

'Well, he has been incredibly kind,' Carrie said. 'After all my parents could never have afforded a place like this, and Diaz has let us live here all this time.' She sighed. 'Although that's coming to an end quite soon, as I expect he told you.'

'No.' Rhianna straightened. 'No, he didn't mention it. But we're hardly on those terms.'

'Oh.' Carrie looked at her, dismayed. 'I thought maybe things had improved a little in that quarter—especially as he offered to fetch you from the station. Simon volunteered, naturally, but Diaz reminded him he was supposed to be getting his hair cut in Falmouth, and said he'd go instead.'

'Yet another of his many acts of kindness,' Rhianna commented unsmilingly. 'So, what's happening about the house?'

Carrie shrugged. 'Apparently he's coming back here. To settle, would you believe? Mother thought, from something he said in passing, that he might be getting married, but there doesn't seem much sign of it. No announcement, and he certainly isn't bringing anyone to the wedding. In fact he may not even stay for it himself. Not with his new toy to play with.'

'Toy?'

'His boat.' Carrie rolled her eyes. '*Windhover* the Wonder Yacht. Or that's how Dad describes it. Like the best kind of floating hotel suite, but powered by a massive engine and moored down at Polkernick. He brought it round from Falmouth the day before yesterday and he's sleeping on board, which has saved Ma having hysterics over the bedroom arrangements here, because usually it's all change when Diaz comes to stay, and as he wasn't expected there'd have been uproar.'

'Of course,' Rhianna said. 'The master must have the master bedroom—however inconvenient.'

But at least this boat might keep him at a distance, she thought. Maybe that's where he was driving off to just now? I can but hope.

'Well,' Carrie said tolerantly, 'you can hardly blame him for wanting his own space. It is his home, after all, even if he hasn't spent that much time here in the past. And now, to Ma's horror, he wants it back, and she'll have to give up being Lady of the Manor.' She grimaced. 'Which she'll hate.'

But she'll go down fighting, Rhianna thought, remembering Moira Seymour's bleak gaze meeting hers a short while ago, from the sofa in the drawing room where she'd sat, poised and chilly as ever, in a silence that had been almost tangible.

'Ah, Miss Carlow.' The cut-glass voice had not changed either. 'I trust you had a pleasant journey?' She'd added coldly, 'Caroline tells me she has put you in the primrose room.'

All the attics full, are they? Rhianna had asked silently. The oubliette filled in?

However, she'd smiled, and said, with her best Lady Ariadne drawl, 'It sounds delightful, Mrs Seymour. I'm so glad to be here.'

Then she had turned, still smiling, to the woman sitting opposite. 'Mrs Rawlins, how lovely to see you again. You're looking well.'

Not that it was true. Widowhood had put years and weight on Simon's mother, and given her mouth a sour turn.

'I hear you're making a name for yourself on television, Rhianna?' As opposed to soliciting at Kings Cross, her tone suggested. 'I find so few programmes of any substance these days that I tend to watch very rarely, of course.'

'Of course,' Rhianna had echoed gently.

'Tea will be served in half an hour, Caroline,' her mother had said. 'Please bring your guest to join us,' she'd added, after a brief hesitation.

Rhianna had been glad to escape upstairs to the designated 'primrose room', which turned out to be as charming as its name suggested, its creamy wallpaper and curtains patterned with sprigs of the tiny flowers, and the bed covered in a pretty shade of leaf-green.

Moira Seymour might not be her favourite person, but Rhianna couldn't fault her choice of décor.

Now, she said slowly, 'Your mother's bound to find leaving here a wrench. But it's an awfully big house for two people.'

'True,' Carrie agreed. 'But an even bigger one for a determined bachelor like Diaz. Unless, of course, he does intend to bite the bullet and become a family man.' She paused. 'Did you ever see him with anyone in particular? The times you ran across him in London, that is?'

Rhianna stared at her. She said jerkily, 'Did he tell you we'd met there?'

'He mentioned you'd been at some bash together.' Carrie shrugged. 'Something to do with insurance?'

'Apex, the company sponsoring *Castle Pride*.' Rhianna nodded. 'But it was a very crowded room, so I didn't notice if he had a companion.' *My first lie.*

'And you were both at a first night party for a new play, weren't you?'

'Perhaps. I don't recall.' Rhianna was casually dismissive as she put away the last of her things. She looked at her watch. 'Now, I suppose we'd better go down to the promised tea. But you'd better explain to me first why the swords are crossed and the daggers drawn. I thought Margaret Rawlins and your mother were friends?'

Carrie sighed. 'They were never that close,' she admitted. 'You see, the Rawlins' cottage was originally a second home, and Ma doesn't approve of such things. Cornwall for the Cornish and all that—even though she and Aunt Esther were both Londoners. And the fact that Mrs Rawlins has now moved down here permanently hasn't altered a thing.'

'But that can't be all, surely?'

'No.' Carrie pulled a face. 'When we began discussing wedding plans Margaret opted out completely. Said that whatever we decided would be fine with her. So—we went ahead.'

'Except she changed her mind?' Rhianna guessed.

'And how,' Carrie said fervently. She began to tick off on her fingers. 'We agreed on the guest lists ages ago, but each time we put the numbers in to the caterers she came up with someone else who simply must be invited. That's probably why she's here today—with yet another afterthought. And that's not all. She thought the charge for the marquee was extortionate and insisted we get another quote from a firm she knew, with the result that someone else hired the one I really wanted. Then, last week, Margaret asked with a sad smile if "Lead Kindly Light" could be one of the hymns, because it was "my poor Clive's favourite."' She shook her head. 'It's beautiful, I know, but hardly celebratory. Besides which, all the Order of Service booklets were printed ages ago.'

She took a deep breath. 'There—that's off my chest. Until the next instalment, anyway. And I know there's going to be one. I feel it.'

'Oh God.' Rhianna looked at her with fascinated horror. 'Couldn't Simon have a word with her?'

Carrie sighed again. 'I asked, but Simon's very defensive about his mother. Says she's still mourning his father, which I'm sure is true, and that we must make allowances—especially as we'll be moving so far away.' She paused. 'Anyway, as I said, he seems in a world of his own these days.'

'Oh?' Rhianna picked up her brush and stroked it carefully through her hair, meeting her own watchful gaze in the mirror. 'In what way?'

'Like nearly missing today's hair appointment, for one thing,' Carrie said ruefully. 'And a few times lately I've arranged to ring him at his flat, only he hasn't been there. Says he forgot, and has stuff of his own to do, anyway.'

'Probably hung over after his stag night and doesn't want to admit it,' Rhianna said lightly.

Carrie stared at her. 'But his stag party was ages ago. He went to Nassau with a bunch of guys from work. They got this special deal and stayed for a couple of extra days. Surely I told you?'

'Yes,' Rhianna said. 'Yes, of course you did. I'm an idiot.'

How could I forget? How could I possibly forget the trip to Nassau, when it was only a couple of days later that I found out about the baby?

She put down the brush, aware that her colour had risen swiftly, guiltily, again.

'I keep telling myself that it doesn't matter,' Carrie went on. 'That it will all be over soon and Simon and I will be on our own, making a new life for ourselves. That I'll look back and laugh at all these niggles. Only…'

'Only just for now you'd like to punch Mrs Rawlins' lights out,' Rhianna supplied briskly. 'Perfectly understandable—even commendable.'

'Oh, Rhianna.' Smiling, Carrie slipped an arm through hers. 'Thank heavens you're here. Nothing is going to seem as bad from now on.'

Oh, God, Rhianna thought, her stomach churning as they went downstairs. I just hope and pray that's true.

Her uneasiness increased when the first person she saw in the drawing room was Diaz, lounging in a chair by the open French windows, glancing through a magazine. The new toy, apparently, wasn't as compelling as she'd hoped.

As they came in he rose politely and smiled, but his eyes, slanting a glance at Rhianna, were as hard a grey as Cornish granite. She made herself walk calmly past him, choosing a deep easy chair where he'd be out of her sightline.

But not, unfortunately, eliminated from her consciousness. She was still as aware of him, of his silent, forbidding presence, as if he'd come to stand beside her, his hand on her shoulder.

She had also placed herself at a deliberately discreet distance from the sofas, where the two mothers were ensconced opposite each other—tacitly acknowledging her position as the outsider in this family gathering, but not so far away that she didn't notice there was now a large, flat box beside Margaret Rawlins and wonder about it. But not for long.

'Caroline, dear,' Mrs Rawlins said, as her future daughter-in-law obediently took a seat beside her mother. 'I was thinking the other day of that old rhyme, "Something old, something new…" and I remembered the very thing. I wore it at my wedding and kept it ever since—thinking, I suppose, that one day I'd have a daughter. But that wasn't to be, of course. So I'd like you to carry on the tradition instead.'

She lifted the lid of the box and carefully extracted from the folds of tissue paper inside a mass of white tulle, layer after layer of it, and a headdress shaped like an elaborate coronet, each of its ornamental stems crowned by a large artificial pearl.

It looked, Rhianna thought dispassionately, like something the Wicked Queen might wear in a remake of Disney's *Snow White*. Only not as good.

In the terrible silence that followed, she did not dare look at Carrie.

Eventually, Carrie said slowly, 'Well, it's a lovely thought, but I wasn't actually intending to wear a veil, just some fresh flowers in my hair. Didn't I explain that?'

'Ah, but a bridal outfit is incomplete without a veil,' said Mrs Rawlins brightly. 'And although I'm sure your dress is very fashionable and modern, I know Simon is quite old-fashioned at heart, and he will like to see you in something rather more conventional too.'

She paused. 'You'll have to be very careful with the coronet, of course. It's extremely delicate, and one of the stems is already a little loose.'

Rhianna found herself looking at Margaret Rawlins with fascination and some bewilderment. She recalled Simon's mother as a perfectly pleasant woman, a good cook and devoted to her family, who had joined in all the local activities with open enjoyment.

So how on earth had she come to turn into the Control Monster?

As for her comments about Simon…

Was it 'old-fashioned' and 'conventional' for a bridegroom to have been sleeping with someone else for the past three months? Telling that someone else that he loved her? Inventing that special deal in the Bahamas in order to be with her for a few stolen days? And eventually committing the overwhelming error of making her pregnant?

My God, she thought, a tiny bubble of hysteria welling up inside her. What a truly great tradition to uphold.

She glanced at Carrie and saw her looking anguished, while Moira Seymour's mouth was tight with outrage.

And then the door opened, and Mrs Henderson came in pushing a laden trolley. The tension, perforce, subsided—if only temporarily.

It helped that it was a superb tea, with plates of tiny crustless sandwiches, a platter of scones still warm from the oven, accompanied by a large bowl of clotted cream and a dish of homemade strawberry jam, together with a featherlight Victoria sponge and a large, rich fruitcake.

Mrs Rawlins fussed endlessly about getting the veil back into its protective wrappings before any of it was served—much to Rhianna's regret. A well-aimed cup of tea would obviously have solved that particular problem for good.

So she'd have to think of something else.

As she returned her tea things to the trolley, she casually picked up the coronet and carried it over to the French windows, as if to examine it more closely.

'Oh, do be careful.' Mrs Rawlins' voice followed her. 'As I've said, one of the stems is very fragile.'

'So it is, but I'm sure I can fix that,' Rhianna said brightly, as her fingers discovered that the stem in question had actually become partly detached from the base.

Well, I'm already the least favourite guest, she thought, so what have I to lose? And she gave it a sharp and effective tweak, before gasping loudly in dismay and turning contritely back to the owner.

'Oh, heavens, it's come off altogether now.' Her voice quivered in distress. 'I'm terribly sorry, Mrs Rawlins. I can't believe I could be so clumsy.'

'Let me see it at once.' Margaret Rawlins was on her feet, her face furiously and unbecomingly flushed. 'Perhaps it can be repaired.'

'I doubt it very much.' Diaz had risen too, unexpectedly, and was crossing to Rhianna's side, taking the mutilated object from her hand. 'It looks seriously broken to me. But it's probably better for this to happen now instead of during the ceremony. That would have been really embarrassing.' The smile he turned on the agitated Mrs Rawlins was charm personified. 'Don't you agree?'

'I suppose so,' the older woman returned after a pause, lips compressed. 'But I don't know what Simon will say when he hears.'

Rhianna stared down at the carpet, as if abashed, her long lashes veiling the sudden flare of anger in her eyes. Simon, she thought grimly, has other things on his mind to worry about.

Fussily, Mrs Rawlins picked up the box with the veil. 'You had better take this upstairs, Caroline—before there's another accident,' she added, with a fulminating glance at Rhianna.

'Yes,' Carrie said without enthusiasm. 'Yes, of course.' She glanced appealingly at Rhianna, who picked up the cue and immediately followed her.

'You're a star,' Carrie said simply, tossing the box onto the bed in her room. 'But what the hell am I going to do with a thousand yards of dead white tulle when I'm wearing ivory satin? Look.'

The dress was lovely, Rhianna thought instantly as it was removed from its protective cover and displayed. A simple Empire line sheath, needing no other adornment but Carrie's charming figure inside it.

She considered. 'What flowers are you wearing in your hair?'

'Roses,' Carrie said. 'Gold and cream, like my bouquet.' She took the veil from the box and lifted it up. 'But they won't be substantial enough to hold a weight like this.'

'Then we'll just have to make it manageable.' Rhianna paused. 'Got a sharp pair of scissors handy?'

'Oh, God,' said Carrie. 'What are you going to do?'

'Cement my reputation as the arch-vandal of the western world,' Rhianna told her cheerfully. 'Simon's mother will never speak to me again, of course, but that's a small sacrifice to make.'

Besides, she would have far more powerful reasons to hate me—if she knew...

She took the veil from Carrie and placed it on her own head, studying herself in the full-length mirror. 'Heavens, it swamps me—and I'm taller than you. However, if we just use one layer we'll be able to see your hair through the tulle, and the flowers will help too, of course. Besides, if I'm careful, it can all be sewn back together afterwards,' she added, grinning, and gave Carrie an encouraging push towards the door. 'Now—scissors and sewing kit.'

Left alone, she picked up the dress with immense care and held it in front of her to see the whole effect. She'd use the veil's shortest tier, she thought, as it would only reach Carrie's shoulders and therefore wouldn't detract from the lovely simplicity of the dress itself.

At least she hoped so. After all, she'd had enough costumes practically re-made on her to know what worked and what didn't, she thought drily.

Then paused, staring at herself, suddenly stricken, as she asked herself what she was doing. Why was she taking this trouble over a wedding that shouldn't even be happening? How she could be helping her friend marry a man who had already betrayed her so terribly?

Especially when there was no guarantee that it would never occur again, she thought bitterly. That Simon would suddenly become repentant and faithful.

But he was the husband Carrie had always wanted—had set her heart on from young girlhood. Had waited for. And this wedding was going to be the culmination of all her sweetest dreams.

The image in the mirror was suddenly blurred. Rhianna lifted a hand and quickly wiped away her tears before they could fall on the precious satin. Besides, she thought she heard a movement in the passage outside, and she couldn't risk Carrie coming back to catch her weeping.

Nor could she take the dream of her friend's whole life and smash it. She would have to keep the secret. Pretend she had no idea there had been a hidden love affair. No baby so soon and so finally eliminated from the equation.

And no dream for me, either, she told herself, pain twisting inside her as she put the dress gently back on its padded hanger and covered it.

Out of all that had happened, she thought, that was the hardest thing to bear. Knowing that she had nothing left to hope for.

And having to live with that knowledge for the rest of her life.

CHAPTER THREE

IT OCCURRED to Rhianna that an excuse to stay out of harm's way in her room was exactly what she'd needed, giving her a chance to catch her breath and regain some of her composure.

Working with immense care, she'd reduced the mass of tulle by two thirds, and the discarded lengths, their raw edges neatly hemmed, were back in the box.

Carrie was reluctantly reconciled to the idea of the shortened version, and by the time Simon's mother discovered what had been done it would be too late. Although the fact that the veil could be subsequently reconstituted in all its voluminous glory might mollify her a little.

Whatever, thought Rhianna. Carrie and I will be long gone anyway, so she'll have to fulminate alone.

But now the time was fast approaching for the next ordeal— a quiet dinner at home with the family. Including, of course, the master of the house.

'The big party's tomorrow evening,' Carrie had told her happily. 'At the Polkernick Arms. We've practically taken the place over.'

Her face had clouded slightly. 'But Simon can't be with us tonight. His godfather and his wife are travelling down from Worcestershire a day early, and Margaret's insisted that he spends the evening at home with them.'

Rhianna had given an inward sigh of relief. At some point, sooner or later, she and Simon would have to face each other, of course. But she'd prefer that to be much, much later.

But his absence was not going to make the occasion any easier for her. Because he was not her only problem, she reminded herself unhappily. There was also Diaz to be confronted yet again, and although there might have been a brief moment's complicity between them in the drawing room earlier, it had been no more than that, and she was totally deluding herself if she believed otherwise.

He would still be gunning for her. Watching her. Waiting for her to make one false move.

So she would have to make damned sure that he was disappointed, she told herself grimly.

And she was armoured for the challenge.

She'd showered, and changed into a silky skirt the colour of indigo, stopped with a white Victorian-style blouse, high-necked and pin-tucked. Demureness itself.

She'd drawn her hair back from her face, securing it at the nape of her neck with a silver clasp, and used the lightest of make-up—a coating of mascara to her long lashes and a touch of colour on her mouth. Nothing more.

She'd accentuated the body lotion used after her shower with a drift of the same fragrance on her throat and wrists, and fixed modest silver studs in her ears.

Neat, she thought, scrutinising herself in the mirror, but not gaudy.

She walked over to the window seat to repack Carrie's sewing basket, and stood for a moment staring out of the window at the grassy headland, the blue ripple of the sea beyond.

It was the last time she would see it like this, because first thing tomorrow they were coming to put up the marquee. So she would take a long, final look now at this view, so familiar and yet at the same time so alien.

So many memories too, she thought wryly, and so few of them to be treasured. In fact, she could almost count them on the fingers of one hand. The feel of the short turf, cool beneath her bare feet as she ran. The hot gritty slide of the sand under her burrowing toes down in the cove, and the eventual, blessed shock of the sea against her heated skin. Misty mornings. Blistering afternoons, lying languid in the shade. All pure nostalgia.

But also tears scalding her eyes, like salt in her throat. And a man's voice saying almost gently, 'What's wrong? There must be something...'

She stirred restlessly. That particular recollection had to go. It had no place in her memory. Not any more.

Perhaps this was really why she was here? she thought. To clear her mind of the past and prepare for a future that in so many ways was looking good. The kind of career many actresses her age could only dream of.

Except her dreams were different, and that was something she had to deal with once and for all.

To accept that she'd been crying for the moon all these years, and that the man she wanted had his own obligations, his own priorities, creating a void between them that could never be crossed.

She turned abruptly away from the window. Took several deep, steadying breaths from her diaphragm, as she did before she began an important scene. She opened her door, stepping into the passage—and ran straight into Simon.

'So there you are.' Abruptly he took her arm, propelling her back into her room and following. 'What's going on, Rhianna? I thought you weren't going to be here. That's what you let me believe, anyway.'

'I told you I hadn't made a decision,' she defended, rubbing the arm he'd grabbed, aware that she was quivering inside, and a lot of it was temper. 'What's the matter, Simon? Conscience troubling you at last?'

'Oh, for God's sake.' His voice was harsh, goaded. 'I made a mistake, that's all. I'm not the first man and I won't be the last to get spooked by the thought of marriage and have a fling before the gates finally shut.'

'A fling?' she echoed bitterly. 'Is that what you call it? It's rather more than that when you tell someone you love her. Make her believe in happy ever after, then dump her, leaving her pregnant with a child she thought you wanted too.'

'Is that why you're here?' he said hoarsely. 'To tell me the termination's been cancelled after all? Or to make some other kind of trouble?'

'No,' she said. 'And—no. Does that put your mind at rest? But understand this, Simon. I'm keeping quiet about this whole hideous mess for Carrie's sake, not yours. You don't deserve her, you appalling creep, and you never have. But you're what she wants.'

'Well,' he said softly, 'she isn't the only one—is she, sweetpea?' He lifted his hand and stroked it insolently down her cheek.

Rhianna flinched away as if she'd been burned. 'Just get out of here,' she said harshly. 'And you'd better make Carrie happy, that's all. Don't ruin her life as well, you complete and utter swine.'

'No,' he said, suddenly sober. 'I won't. Because I really do love her. Maybe it took a stupid, meaningless involvement to teach me how much. To make me realise I couldn't bear to lose her. Can you understand that?'

'I'll never understand you, Simon.' Her glance was cold and level. 'Or anything that's happened in the last months. Not if I live to be a thousand.' She paused. 'And my own loss, of course, doesn't matter,' she added bitterly.

'Come off it, Rhianna.' The mockery was back, coupled with a note of triumph. 'How can you lose what you never had? Get real.' He paused. 'And now, sadly, I must tear myself away. But I'll be back tomorrow, so remember that I'm about to marry your best friend and be nice, hmm?' He gave her a valedictory grin, and departed.

Left alone, Rhianna sank down on the edge of the bed, feeling the inner trembling spread through her body, permeating every nerve, every sinew.

Calm down, she told herself. You've seen Simon. Spoken to him. You don't have to do that again. By now he'll be gone. Tomorrow there'll be a mad rush to get everything done, and avoiding him should be pretty easy. The trick is not to make it too obvious, or Carrie will notice and wonder.

Tonight, you'll simply be—pleasant, speaking only when spoken to. You know how to do that. God knows, you've had plenty of practice over the years, right here in this house, where you'll always be the interloper. The unwanted guest.

And when dinner's over you can yawn, say you're tired after the journey. Make that your excuse for an early night.

But above all you will not—*not*—cry. Certainly not now. But not even tonight, when it's dark, and you're lying on your own, thinking of—him. Trying not to want him and failing miserably. Just as you've done for so many nights in the past. As you'll want to do for the rest of your life.

Having composed herself with an effort before venturing downstairs again, it was something of an anti-climax to walk into the drawing room, her head high, and find it empty.

But the rest of the party were clearly expected, because a tray of drinks, including large jugs of Pimms and home-made lemonade, plus a cooler containing white wine, had been set out on a side table.

The French windows were standing open, and the evening sun was pouring into the room like warm gold, accompanied by the faint whisper of the sea like a siren call.

Rhianna took two steps towards the open air, then paused. However pressing her desire to escape, she was hardly dressed for scrambling over rocks and sand, or for paddling through the creaming shallows of the tide, she reminded herself drily. Far better to stand her ground and hope the evening would pass quickly.

She wandered back towards the wide stone fireplace, and stood looking up at the portraits which flanked it of Tamsin Penvarnon and her Spanish husband.

Carrie had told her all about them one afternoon, when they'd been alone because Simon had been dragged unwillingly to Truro, shopping with his mother.

'Several years after the Armada there was a Spanish raid on Cornwall,' she'd said. 'They burnt Mousehole and Newlyn, but as they were getting away in their galleys there was a fight, and one of their marine captains, Jorge Diaz, was wounded and swept overboard. He was washed up in our cove and Tamsin Penvarnon, the family's only daughter, found him there, half drowned. She had him carried up to the house and nursed him until he recovered.'

She gave an impish grin. 'Then Tamsin found she was having a baby. So she and Captain Diaz got married—only the family put it about that he was really her cousin, one of the Black

Penvarnons from near St Just, in case anyone asked awkward questions. He took the family name, but he and Tamsin called one of their sons Diaz, and the tradition has kept going ever since. So when Uncle Ben and Aunt Esther had a boy, everyone knew what he'd be christened.'

She sighed. 'It's a wonderful story—especially as it turned out that Jorge Diaz's father was one of the *conquistadores* who went to South America and won lots of land and masses of gold, which he left to Jorge's elder brother, Juan. But Juan Diaz got fever and died too, so everything came to Jorge and Tamsin, which is how the Penvarnon fortune started. And, to add to it all, they found enormous mineral deposits on their estates in Chile. Which is why my cousin Diaz is a multimillionaire and we're the poor relations,' she added buoyantly. 'Only Mummy doesn't like me to say that.'

Rhianna digested this. 'Is Mrs Penvarnon—your aunt—dead too?'

'Oh, no.' Carrie shook her head. 'She lives abroad. She just—doesn't come back here.'

'Why not—when it's so beautiful?'

Carrie shrugged. 'I asked Daddy once, and he said that though Mummy and Aunt Esther were both Londoners, some people didn't transplant as well as others. Although Jorge Diaz seemed to manage it,' she added. 'He and Tamsin had their portraits painted when they got rich, and she's wearing the Penvarnon necklace, all gold and turquoise, that he had made for her. Their pictures are in the drawing rooms. One day when no one's around I'll show them to you.'

Carrie had been as good as her word, Rhianna recalled, and she'd stood enthralled as she gazed up at the long-ago lovers—he with the kind of saturnine good-looks to die for, and she a red-gold beauty with vivid blue eyes.

Now, as she took another look, the resemblance between Diaz Penvarnon and his Spanish ancestor was truly amazing, she acknowledged with reluctance once again. Shave the black pointed beard, replace the snowy ruff with an open-necked shirt and substitute a mobile phone for the sword Don Jorge's hand was resting on with such stunning authority, and they could be twins.

Both of them adventurers too, she thought. Their eyes looking outward with challenge, seeking new worlds to conquer and fresh fortunes to be made.

Had Tamsin known what she was taking on that day in the cove? she wondered. Or had she ever sighed for a more settled existence?

She moved slightly closer. Tamsin hadn't the expression of a lady who suffered from doubts. Her eyes and faint smile held the same proud certainty as that of her husband. One hand toyed with an elaborate feathered fan, while the other pointed beringed fingers at the dramatic chain of turquoises, set in gold, that surrounded her neck, its single pendant stone, encircled by pearls, nestling enticingly in the valley between her breasts.

'It used to be kept in that display case over there on the table,' Carrie had told her, as they'd stood gazing that first time. 'But there were problems with insurance, so Uncle Ben decided it should live in the bank. Penvarnon brides always wear it on their wedding days, so I suppose we'll have to wait for Diaz to get married before it comes out again.' She'd darted across the room to the table in question. 'But the fan's still here, if you want to have a look.'

I should have stuck at looking, Rhianna recalled ruefully, but the temptation to take the lovely thing from its satin bed and hold it had been too strong.

And as she'd touched it something strange had happened to her, as if the simple action of unfurling a fan and waving it smoothly and languidly had transformed her into a different person—a grown woman, aware of the power of her own beauty. She'd moved slowly across the room, her walk a glide, glancing from left to right under her lashes, as if acknowledging the admiration she aroused.

She'd thought since that that was the moment when she'd known with absolute certainty she would become an actress. That she might be able to hide from her intrinsic loneliness by becoming other people.

At the time, she'd spun round on her toe, laughing almost shamefacedly at her own silly fantasies—only to look past Carrie and see Moira Seymour standing grim-faced in the doorway, with Diaz Penvarnon just behind her.

'How dare you?' The older woman's voice had been molten with anger. 'How dare you touch anything in this house, you little—?'

'It's not her fault,' Carrie broke in staunchly. 'I told her she could.'

'Then you had no right, Caroline.' Her mother turned on her furiously. 'This is a Penvarnon family heirloom, not some cheap toy to be passed around and played with. In future, the case will be locked. And this girl should not be in the house, anyway. I gave strict instructions about that.' She took a step forward, her hand outstretched, her eyes fixed inimically on Rhianna's white face. 'Now, give it back and get out. And believe me—you haven't heard the last of this.'

'I haven't done anything to it.' The words came out all wrong. They sounded sullen when she'd meant them to be apologetic and reassuring. 'I wouldn't.' She glanced up at the portrait. 'I just wanted to hold it because it was hers, and she's so beautiful.'

Diaz Penvarnon said with quiet authority, 'It's all right, Aunt Moira. I'll deal with this.' He moved past Mrs Seymour and took the fan carefully from Rhianna's numb fingers.

He said, 'You might not mean to harm it, but it's very old and consequently extremely fragile.' He looked at Mrs Seymour. 'And, as I said when I was last here, it properly belongs in a good costume museum. I shall see to that.'

There was a silence, then Moira Seymour said, openly reluctant, 'Of course—if that is what you wish.'

'Yes,' he said. 'It is.' He replaced the fan gently in the case and closed the glass lid. 'There,' he added. 'No real harm done. Now, off you go, both of you, and we'll say no more about it.'

He'd been as good as his word, Rhianna thought. The expected tongue-lashing from Aunt Kezia had never materialised. And the glass case and its contents had been removed from the drawing room and taken away in a van a few days later.

'Mummy's in a fearful temper about it,' Carrie had reported dolefully. 'She used to like pointing it out to visitors—our genuine Elizabethan relic. And now she can't. And she got even more cross when Daddy said the fan belonged to Diaz's ancestors, not ours, and he was entitled to dispose of it as he saw fit.'

She paused, then looked more cheerful. 'He also said that barring you from the house was the kind of stupid, unkind rule which was bound to be broken, and he was only surprised it hadn't happened before. He said that Diaz thought so too. So we don't have to worry about that any more.'

Rhianna knew they almost certainly did, but kept quiet about it anyway.

Now, all this long time later, nothing had changed, she admitted with an inward sigh. She allowed herself one long, last look at Tamsin, a woman who had fought for and won the man she loved—but not, she thought wryly, without breaking the rules of her own time. Then she turned away—only to halt with a stifled gasp.

Diaz was standing in the French windows, one shoulder negligently propped against the frame as he watched her silently.

She said unevenly, 'You—you startled me.'

'Not as much as I'd hoped,' he said. 'Or you'd have stayed away.'

Rhianna bit her lip. She said tautly, 'I meant that I didn't know you were there.'

'You were lost in thought,' he said. 'Clearly those portraits fascinate you just as much now as they seemed to when you were a child.'

She shrugged. 'They tell a fascinating story.' She paused. 'And that's an amazing necklace. I wonder why he chose to give her turquoises?'

'The turquoise is said to represent the connection between the sky and the sea,' he said. 'Which makes it an appropriate stone for a Cornishwoman.'

'Ah,' she said. 'Well, I was rather hoping you'd lend it to Carrie for her wedding, so I'd get the chance to see it in reality.'

'I'm sorry,' he said, without a hint of regret. 'It's to be worn by Penvarnon brides only, as a symbol of constancy and faithfulness in marriage.' His brief smile was unamused. 'Which rather puts it out of the running—wouldn't you say?'

'I think Carrie would be a loyal and wonderful wife for any man,' Rhianna said.

'Of course,' he said. 'I was actually referring to the groom, in this instance, as I'm sure you of all people should realise.'

She didn't look at him. 'Whatever. The decision is yours, naturally. And, as I can't see myself on the guest list when you tie the knot, I'll just have to resign myself to admiring the necklace only through oil on canvas.' She paused again. 'I hope the fan found a good home in the end?'

'Ah, yes,' he said. 'With so much else going on I'd almost forgotten about that particular incident. However, I can assure you that it has indeed been well taken care of ever since.'

He walked forward into the room. 'But I'm forgetting my duties as host, and that will never do,' he added courteously. 'May I get you a drink? Some Pimms, perhaps?'

It was the perfect drink for a warm evening, and Rhianna longed to say yes, but common sense warned that she needed to keep her wits about her, unclouded by alcohol.

She said, 'Thank you, but I think I'll stick to lemonade.'

There was an odd pause. He looked at her, his mouth hardening, then said, 'Yes—of course,' turning almost abruptly to the drinks tray.

Ice cubes chinked in the tall glass as he poured the lemonade and brought it to her.

'So, what shall we drink to?' He raised his own glass in a parody of a toast. 'Our happy couple? Or your continued good health? More necessary than ever now, I should imagine.'

Rhianna's brows lifted sharply. 'Why do you say that?'

He shrugged. 'The shooting schedule for your series must be fairly hectic. You couldn't afford a lengthy absence for any reason—especially when there must be dozens of other pretty faces manoeuvring to take your place in front of the camera.'

'Thank you for reminding me. I expect there are hundreds.' The lemonade, cold and tangy without bitterness, soothed the dryness of her mouth. 'But I manage to stay reasonably fit. I won't need a replacement yet awhile.'

'But there's bound to come a time when that will happen,' Diaz countered. 'The viewing public is notoriously fickle in its affections. So, will there be life after *Castle Pride*?'

'I'm touched by your concern,' she said curtly. 'However, I'm not ready for the scrapheap in the foreseeable future. Unless you've bought a controlling share in the production company, of course, and even then you'd have a fight on your hands.'

'No,' he said softly. 'You're not the type to go quietly, Rhianna. You've made that more than clear.'

There was something in his voice that sent all her antennae quivering again. But as she stared at him, questions tumbling around in her head, the door opened and Carrie came in, face flushed and eyes sparkling. But not with happiness.

'I don't believe it,' she burst out furiously. 'I just don't. After everything else—now this!'

'What's happened?' Rhianna moved to her swiftly.

'Mrs Rawlins,' said Carrie, in a voice that managed to combine anger with despair. '*She's* happened—again.'

'Don't tell me,' Rhianna said quickly, trying to coax her to smile. 'She's found out about the veil and she's planning to sue.'

But Carrie was not to be cajoled. 'She informed us before she left that she'd invited Simon's godparents specially early so that they could come out to dinner with us tomorrow—in order to meet everybody. And said how much they were looking forward to it.'

She spread her hands dramatically. 'Mother immediately explained that the Polkernick Arms can only seat so many people, but she said that she was sure if we all squeezed up a little they could accommodate two more. But they can't, and they won't. I know it.'

Rhianna gave her a comforting hug. 'Well, Simon will just have to talk to his mother. Make her see reason.'

'Unlikely,' Carrie said with unusual brusqueness. 'She's already persuaded him that the guest list is heavily loaded in our family's favour. He'll say we have to fit them in, even if it means cancelling the Arms and finding a bigger restaurant. Something that's already been hinted at,' she added on a note of doom. 'But there's nowhere—not at this late stage anyway.'

They were joined by Moira Seymour, looking thoroughly harassed. 'The manageress won't budge.' She addressed Carrie. 'We're already at the maximum the regulations allow, as I tried to tell that impossible woman earlier. What on earth are we going to do? We can't ask other people to drop out to make room for them.'

'No,' Diaz said unexpectedly. 'But in an emergency you can

always find volunteers.' He looked at Rhianna, his mouth smiling coolly. 'Well, Miss Carlow,' he said softly. 'Will you help save the situation for Carrie tomorrow evening by giving up the party and having dinner on your own with me instead? What do you say?'

There was the kind of silence that seemed to last for ever.

Bombshell at the end of Act Two, Rhianna thought, with a kind of detachment. Cast reaction, followed by slow curtain. Old-fashioned, but effective.

For instance, she could see that Carrie's mouth had formed into an 'o' of pure astonishment, while her mother appeared to have turned into an ice sculpture. She found that she herself had become rooted to the spot, bereft of words, but numbingly aware of the mockery in Diaz Penvarnon's grey eyes as he watched her. Waiting for her response.

Moira Seymour found her voice first. 'But that's quite impossible,' she declared. 'It's awfully good of you, of course, Diaz, but you're Carrie's cousin. She's being married from your house. You can't possibly miss the family dinner.'

'If you recall, it was by no means certain that I was even coming to the wedding.' Diaz's tone was dry. 'And I doubt I'll be here for the ceremony even now. But the occasion will still go ahead without me.' He paused. 'And I believe Rhianna was a late entry to the guest list too,' he added gently. 'Which would seem to make us an ideal pairing.'

'Except that it's totally absurd,' Moira Seymour said angrily. 'You can't possibly want…' She paused, as if realising her next comment might be infelicitous. 'I mean, I can't allow you to sacrifice yourself like this, my dear Diaz. Miss Carlow—Rhianna—wouldn't expect it.'

'Please don't regard me as some kind of victim.' He sounded amused. 'Perhaps you don't realise there isn't a man in England who wouldn't jump at the chance of dinner *à deux* with television's top fantasy woman.'

Isn't there? thought Rhianna. *Isn't there?* Because I can think of one standing only a few feet away right now. So why are you doing this? *Why?*

'Besides, just think of the moral victory you'll score over

Margaret Rawlins,' he went on. 'Arming for a battle and finding it's been cancelled. All the Brownie points for good behaviour to our side, and only at the cost of two new place-cards.'

He turned to Rhianna. 'I know you must be disappointed at missing out, but comfort yourself with the knowledge that you've headed off yet another difficulty at this happy time, and can bask in the bridegroom's undying gratitude.'

He allowed an instant's silence for her to digest this, then smiled at her charmingly. 'So, are you prepared to make this sacrifice, Rhianna—for Simon's sake, if nothing else?'

She met his gaze, hard and metallic, like silver. Read its challenge, which held no charm at all.

'Put like that,' she said coldly and clearly, 'how can I possibly refuse?'

His smile widened. 'Oh, I'm sure we can both think of a number of ways,' he said softly.

He turned to Moira Seymour, whose expression was still set in stone. 'I suggest Rhianna goes with you to the hotel for a token appearance at the pre-dinner drinks, which will thrill the *Castle Pride* fans, and then I'll whisk her away before the management start counting heads. Agreed?'

'I suppose so.' It was Carrie who spoke, her tone reluctant. She walked over to Rhianna and slid an arm through hers. 'Although it's the last thing I'd planned—to have two of my favourite people missing.' She frowned fiercely. 'But it's a solution to a problem that should never have arisen, and I shall tell Simon so.'

'Well, don't be too fierce.' Diaz smiled at her. 'Or he might change his mind and not turn up on Saturday.'

She relaxed, grinning back at him. 'Never in this world,' she said.

While Rhianna, her own face expressionless, drank some lemonade and felt it turn to pure acid in her throat.

CHAPTER FOUR

THE dinner that followed was not the easiest Rhianna had ever sat through, although the watercress soup, the ducklings with kumquats, and the crème brûlée which rounded off the meal were all flawless.

At another time she'd have been irritated by Moira Seymour's faintly fretful monologue about the wedding, and the problems arising from it, all attributable to Margaret Rawlins, a subject from which she refused to be diverted despite her husband and daughter's best efforts.

But Rhianna was simply thankful not to be required either to contribute or even to listen.

On the other hand, she realised tautly, an absorbing conversation on some neutral topic might have proved a distraction from the presence of Diaz, equally silent, on the other side of the table.

When coffee had been drunk he excused himself, pausing briefly beside Rhianna's chair on his way to the door. His brief smile did not reach his eyes. 'Until tomorrow evening, then. At the hotel.'

She made herself look back at him. 'Yes,' she said. 'Of course. Until then.'

And only she was aware that the hand replacing her cup on its saucer was not entirely steady.

'You didn't eat much at dinner,' Carrie commented critically, as the pair of them walked on the headland later, enjoying the cool, moonlit stillness. 'But be warned—you're not allowed to be ill—not just before my big day.'

'I think I'm just a little tense,' Rhianna admitted, trying to inject some lightness into her tone. 'Thinking more about tomorrow night's meal instead.'

'It'll be fine,' Carrie consoled her. 'In fact, though I hate to admit it, you'll probably be far better off elsewhere.' She grimaced. 'This family dinner promises to be tricky in the extreme, accompanied by a strong whiff of burning martyrs. And after all,' she added, 'it's not the first time Diaz has taken you out to dinner *à deux*.'

Rhianna stared at her, her throat tightening. 'What do you mean?'

'Your birthday treat,' Carrie prompted. 'You can't have forgotten the high note of your early teens? I've never been so jealous in my life.'

'No,' Rhianna said quietly after a pause. 'I—hadn't forgotten.' She looked up at the sky. 'I might walk down to the cove before I turn in. I love seeing the moon on the water. Want to come?'

'Not in these heels,' Carrie demurred. 'And you take care, too,' she added severely. 'I'm not having you hobbling into church with a broken ankle either.'

'All right, Granny,' Rhianna said meekly, and dodged, laughing.

A broken ankle would heal, she thought as she made her way down the track. But what do you do about a breaking heart? And how do you prevent the ache of all the lonely years ahead of you?

Shoes in hand, she walked down the beach until she reached a particular flat rock, and sat down, looking at the sea, smooth as glass in the moonlight.

Nothing to be seen this time. No movement in the water. No dark head, sleek and glossy as a seal's, breaking its surface in the glitter of the late afternoon sun of that long-ago day.

Although she'd been too immersed in her own unhappiness to notice anything around her. Or not immediately, anyway.

Her thirteenth birthday, she'd been thinking with desolation. And no one had remembered. She'd received no presents. Not even a card. And Aunt Kezia hadn't even wished her Many happy returns of the day. While Carrie, who would at least have sung 'Happy Birthday', was away on a school field trip.

She'd waited in vain all day for something—anything. A token recognition of this milestone in her young life. Disappointment and hurt had built up inside her as she'd remembered past birthdays.

Her mother had always made them special, she thought. Magical. Parties for her schoolfriends, including more recently a theatre matinee, and a hilarious trip to an ice rink. Always a cake with candles, and the warmth of arms round her. The knowledge that she was loved and treasured.

She'd tried hard to be brave, telling herself it didn't matter that the day had been ignored this time. That next year it would be different. Knowing that it probably wouldn't.

Until eventually she'd escaped down to the cove, the place where she'd been happiest since she arrived at Penvarnon, and once there, sitting on her favourite rock, had found her eyes blurring as she was suddenly tipped over some edge into a morass of loneliness and pain, where tears were the only relief.

And once she'd started to cry it had been impossible to stop, and she'd lain, hunched and shaking with her sobs, on the hard, flat surface.

She'd been pushing herself upright again, hiccupping a little as she tried to drag a strand of drenched hair away from her face, when she saw him.

Saw Diaz Penvarnon emerging from the sea, completely nude, the salt drops glistening on his body as he strode through the shallows to the beach, as unaware of her presence as she'd been of his. Until then.

The sound she had made, however, a small choking cry of shock and embarrassment, had brought his head round sharply, and he'd stared at her, brows snapping together.

He'd said, with a kind of resignation, 'Oh, God,' then walked to the folded towel waiting on a patch of shingle, winding it swiftly round his lower body.

Then he'd walked across to her, grim-faced. 'Rhianna Carlow,' he said. 'What the hell are you doing here?'

'I wanted to be by myself,' she said huskily. Her eyes were

gummed with weeping, and her face was hot with mortification as she pressed her hands to her cheeks. 'I thought all your visitors had gone and you'd left as well.'

'Didn't you see there was someone swimming and figure they might like some privacy too?' he asked harshly, then paused, his attention arrested as he saw her distress. He went on more gently. 'Come on, it's not that bad, surely? You must have seen a man without his clothes before?'

She hadn't, as it happened, but she didn't say so.

'It—it's not that.' She swallowed another sob.

'Then what's wrong?' He was frowning again, but as if he were puzzled rather than angry. 'There must be something.' He sat down beside her, his hand cool and damp on her shoulder through the thin tee shirt. 'Don't cry any more. Tell me.'

She bent her head, her voice catching on the words. 'It's my birthday—I'm thirteen—and no one remembered…'

He said, almost blankly, 'Dear God.' Then he was silent for so long that she glanced at him, wondering, and saw the tanned face hard and set as he stared at the sea.

She felt nervous again, and moved restively, dislodging his hand. She said haltingly, 'I'm sorry. I'm stopping you getting dressed. I—I'll go. My aunt will be looking for me.'

'Doubtful,' he said. 'In the extreme. But don't run away. I've got an idea that might improve matters.' He added drily, 'And my clothes are in The Cabin, so you don't have to worry. I won't be blighting your adolescence a second time.' He sent her a brief, taut smile. 'So, wait here until I'm decent again, and we'll walk back to the house together.'

She had a belated but pretty fair idea of what she must look like, and was tempted to ignore his instructions and bolt while he was in The Cabin getting dressed. But something told her that he, at least, was trying to be kind, so it was only good manners to wait and hear what he had to say.

She did what she could, scrubbing fiercely at her face with her sodden hanky, and combing her hair with her fingers.

When he came out of The Cabin, she joined him, eyes down, and they walked up the track side by side.

He took her straight round to the stable block, where Miss Trewint was cleaning the paintwork on their front entrance.

She checked, her lips thinning. 'Rhianna, where have you been? I hope and pray you haven't been making a nuisance of yourself again.'

'On the contrary,' Diaz said. 'I found her in the cove, like a sea urchin on a rock, and she's been excellent company. So much so that, with your permission, I'd like to take her out to dinner to celebrate her birthday.'

He paused, and the older woman gazed at him open-mouthed, her face warming with undisguised annoyance.

'Unless you have something else planned, of course,' he added smoothly. 'No? I thought not.' He turned to Rhianna, who was also staring at him, dumbfounded and totally lost for words, but with an odd little tendril of disbelieving joy unfurling inside her too.

'Wash your face, sea urchin,' he directed. 'And I'll be back around six-thirty to collect you.'

Kezia Trewint found her voice. 'Mr Penvarnon, this is nonsense. There's absolutely no need for you to go to all this trouble…'

'Now, there we disagree.' His smile held charm, but it was also inexorable, and Rhianna felt a faint shiver between her shoulder-blades. 'So—six-thirty. Don't be late.' And he was gone.

Alone in the moonlight, Rhianna let herself remember…

Aunt Kezia, of course, had not bothered to disguise her anger and bitterness at this turn of events.

'Barely out of childhood, and already throwing yourself at a man.' She chewed at the words and spat them out. 'And a Penvarnon man at that. The shame of it. And he must have taken leave of his senses.'

'I didn't throw myself,' Rhianna protested. 'He felt sorry for me and was kind. That's all.'

'Because you told him the suffering orphan tale, I suppose? All big eyes and no bread in the house.' Miss Trewint scrubbed at the paintwork as if determined to reach the bare wood beneath it. 'And what will Mrs Seymour have to say when she hears? We'll be lucky to keep our place here.'

Rhianna stared at her. 'Mr Penvarnon wouldn't let us be sent away—not for something he'd done,' she protested.

'So you think you know him that well, do you?' Miss Trewint gave a harsh laugh. 'Well—like mother, like daughter. I should have known.' She paused. 'You'd better get ready, if you're going. You can't keep him waiting.'

Rhianna went up to the flat. Whatever Aunt Kezia said, she thought rebelliously, she wasn't going to allow it to spoil the evening ahead—the prospect of being taken out to dinner as if she was grown-up.

But she couldn't entirely dismiss the older woman's unpleasant remarks, especially when she recalled Carrie's reluctant confidences.

She knew in her heart that Grace Carlow had been a good and loving person, and that she couldn't have—wouldn't have—done anything wrong. All the same there was a mystery there, and one day she would get to the bottom of it and clear her mother's name.

But common sense told her that she must wait until she was older for her questions to be taken seriously.

She had a quick bath and washed her hair, being careful not to use too much hot water, while she mused on what to wear.

She would have given anything to have a cupboard full of the kind of clothes her classmates wore outside school, at the weekends and at holiday times, she thought wistfully, but her aunt considered serviceable shorts and tee shirts, with a pair of jeans for cooler days, an adequate wardrobe for her. And she couldn't even contemplate what Kezia Trewint would have said about the make-up and jewellery the other girls took for granted.

Which only left her school uniform dresses, still relatively new, full-skirted and square necked in pale blue.

Sighing, she put one of them on, slipped her feet into her black regulation shoes, brushed her cloud of hair into relative submission and went downstairs to wait for him.

He was a few minutes late, and for a stricken moment she wondered if he'd had second thoughts. Then he came striding across the stable yard with a set look to his mouth which suggested that Moira Seymour might indeed have had something to say about his plan.

But his face relaxed when he saw her, and he said, 'You're looking good, Miss Carlow. Shall we go?'

His car was wonderful, low, sleek and clearly powerful, but he kept its power strictly harnessed as he negotiated the narrow high-hedged lanes leading out of Polkernick with a sure touch.

It wasn't a long journey—just a few miles down the coast to another village built on a steep hill overlooking a harbour. The restaurant was right on the quay, occupying the upper storey of a large wooden building like a boathouse, and reached by an outside staircase.

Inside, it was equally unpretentious, with plain wooden tables and chairs, and the menu and wine list chalked up on blackboards.

There were quite a few people eating already, but a table for two had been reserved by the window with a view of the harbour, and a girl in tee shirt and jeans came to light the little lamp in its glass shade which stood in middle of the table, and take their order for drinks.

A combination of excitement and her crying jag had made Rhianna thirsty, and she asked shyly for water.

'Bring a jug for both of us, please, Bethan. Ice, but no lemon,' Diaz directed. 'And just a half-bottle of the Chablis I had last time.'

He smiled at Rhianna. 'It's a seafood place,' he said. 'I suppose I should have asked if you like fish.'

'I like everything,' she said simply, adding, 'Except tripe.'

'That's not a taste I've acquired either.' He paused. 'Ever had lobster?'

Mutely, she shook her head.

'Then that's what we'll have,' he said.

And so they did—plain and grilled, with a tossed green salad, a bowl of tiny sauté potatoes, and a platter of fresh, crusty bread. It was preceded by a delicate shrimp mousse, and when the wine came Diaz poured a very small amount into another glass and handed it to her.

'To Rhianna,' he said, raising his own glass. 'On her birthday.'

She sipped the wine carefully, and thought it was like tasting sunshine and flowers.

Her pudding was a raspberry tartlet with clotted cream, carried ceremoniously to the table by a stout man with a large apron over his blue check trousers who, Diaz told her, was the owner and chef, Morris Trencro. In the middle was a tiny ornamental holder, with a lighted candle for her to make a wish, then blow out.

'No room for the proper thirteen, maiden,' Mr Trencro said. 'But reckon you won't mind that.'

What was more, he began singing 'Happy Birthday,' in a strong baritone, and at his signal the rest of the customers joined in, turning to smile at this young red-haired girl whose eyes were shining more brightly than any candle flame.

And then they'd driven home, as decorously as they'd come.

There had been a moon that night too, thought Rhianna, and Diaz had put quiet, beautiful music—Debussy, she thought—on the CD player. And what with that, all the gorgeous food and that little drop of wine, she'd had to fight to stay awake, because she didn't want to miss a single moment of her heavenly evening.

Of course, there had been repercussions later, she recalled wryly. Not from Aunt Kezia, oddly enough, although that was probably due to the brief, private interview Diaz had had with her in the sitting room after he'd brought her home.

But Moira Seymour had seemed to develop another layer of ice whenever she saw her.

And worst of all, she thought, was when she'd returned to school in September and found herself the object of unwanted and unwarranted attention from some of the older girls.

'My sister Bethan saw you at the Boathouse in Garzion with Diaz Penvarnon,' Lynn Dellow had announced, looking Rhianna up and down. 'She says he was making a big fuss about your birthday, and pouring wine down you. She says you were wearing your yucky school dress and looked a proper sight.' She giggled. 'I thought Mr Penvarnon liked ladies his own age, not little schoolgirls.'

'That's a disgusting thing to say,' Rhianna told her hotly. 'It wasn't like that. I—I didn't have many birthday presents, and so he gave me a treat, that's all.'

'Did he try and snog you on the way home?' someone else asked eagerly.

'No.' Shocked and upset, Rhianna felt her face turn the colour of a peony. 'No, of course not. That's rubbish. He wouldn't do anything like that.' And suddenly she remembered the night when she'd inadvertently glimpsed him on the terrace, intimately entwined with that girl, and how it had made her feel. How she'd found herself guiltily wondering what it would be like to be kissed—caressed—in that way by a man...

'Bet you wish he had, though,' said Lynn. She sighed gustily. 'Sex on a stick, that one.'

'Well, you're quite wrong.' Rhianna lifted her chin, dismissing the inconvenient jolt to her memory. 'As it happens, Diaz Penvarnon is the last man in the world I'd ever fancy.'

There was some derisive laughter, and a couple of girls looked at her as if she'd grown an extra head.

'Pretty high and mighty for a nobody, aren't we?' Lynn said critically. 'So who's your dream man, Lady Muckcart?'

Rhianna swallowed. She had to say something—name someone—if only to get them to stop talking about Diaz in that horrible way, which made her burn everywhere all over again.

'Simon Rawlins, actually,' she said, adding, 'If you must know.'

After all, she told herself defensively, it wasn't that much of a lie. Who wouldn't want Simon? And hadn't she been secretly hoping she might run into him in the village again some time?

'That tasty blond bit who comes down here every summer?' Lynn stared at her. 'Lives at the top of the village? Thought he hung around with Carrie Seymour.'

'Not all the time,' Rhianna tossed back over her shoulder, as the bell sounded and she walked away.

'That wouldn't stop her,' she heard someone say. 'Takes after her mother, I dare say.' And there was more laughter.

And she hadn't had the courage to turn back and say, What are you talking about? What do you mean?

But even without that her image of Diaz smiling at her across the table had become blurred, as if it had been touched by a hand dipped in slime.

And her precious birthday celebration had been spoiled—tainted, she thought, with a sigh that was almost a sob.

She recovered herself with a start, and slid down from the rock, smoothing her skirt. Bed for you, my girl, she told herself, with a touch of harshness. Before you get maudlin, remembering a time when he could be kind.

Because tomorrow night, when you have dinner with him for the last time, kindness will be the last thing on his mind and you know it.

Ten years on, at least she didn't have the same problems over her wardrobe, she thought wryly, as she viewed herself in the mirror the following evening.

She'd decided to wear the dress she'd originally planned for that night, a wrap-around style in a dark green silky fabric, which accentuated the colour of her eyes. The skirt reached mid-calf, the sleeves were three-quarter length, and its cross-over bodice revealed a discreet plunge.

She'd slept badly the previous night, and she'd been jumpy all day, thankful for all the tiny last-minute tasks that she'd been able to help with, while all the time she was turning her mind by sheer force of will away from the prospect of the evening ahead of her.

But now the time was nearly here. In less than an hour, she thought, glancing at her watch, she'd be setting off for the Polkernick Arms in one of the taxis that had been ordered.

Where Diaz would be waiting…

She drew a deep breath as she fastened her prettiest earrings—small gold hoops studded with tiny emeralds—into her lobes. She still couldn't fathom the actual motive behind his invitation. If she was feeling charitable, she might attribute it to his wish to solve the Seymours' unexpected problem and save them further embarrassment.

But charity isn't the name of the game, she told herself silently. For either of us.

She took one long, final look, checking that the pink polish on her finger and toenails was still immaculate, and that her make-up was understated but effective.

Then she collected the green patent purse that matched her elegant strappy sandals and went downstairs.

There was the usual momentary hush as she entered the drawing room, and she knew that many of the older people in the room would be looking at her and seeing someone else entirely—her mother, Grace Carlow.

Knew too that someone would be saying in an undertone, 'But you must remember—all that appalling scandal. That's why Esther won't be here. She doesn't come near the place. Hasn't done for years now. Poor Moira must be devastated.'

The devastated Moira simply gave her a look and turned away, but Francis Seymour came over to her with a smile. 'Every inch a star, Rhianna,' he told her kindly. He handed her a glass of pale sherry. 'I hope this is to your taste. You look like a *fino* girl to me.'

She laughed. 'You guessed right.' She raised the glass. 'Here's to the family gathering. I hope it goes well.'

He gave her a dry look. 'I would not put money on it, but we shall see.' He sighed suddenly. 'Sometimes I wish that Carrie hadn't been quite so single-minded about her future. That she'd had other serious boyfriends besides Simon. Oh, I've nothing against the boy. But she was so very young—hardly more than a child—when she decided he was the one, as, of course, you know, which is why I can mention it to you.'

'Yes,' she said. She cleared her throat. 'I think—I believe that sometimes it can happen like that. You meet someone—and you know. And that's it—for ever. No questions. No second thoughts.' She stared down at her glass. 'So then you have to hope that he feels the same.'

She took another steadying breath, praying that her voice would not shake. 'And Simon clearly does, which is why there's going to be a wedding tomorrow.'

'And you, Rhianna?' he said gently. 'When are we going to be invited to your wedding?'

She managed another laugh. 'Oh, I'm an impossible case. Married to my career, as they say. On the other hand, I might meet someone at tomorrow's reception. You never know.'

'No,' he said. He gave her a reflective look. 'Although there was a time when I thought I did.' He paused. 'But now I see my wife beckoning, so I must go.'

Rhianna put down the sherry glass untouched. Carrie's father was a shrewd man, she thought, her stomach churning. What had he been trying to say just then? That he'd once seen something—and guessed how she felt…?

No, she thought. Please, no. Let it stay a secret for just a little while longer. Another twenty-four hours and I'll be gone for good. And no one need ever know—anything.

The initial free-for-all at the Polkernick Arms had some of the overtones of the Montagues versus the Capulets, Rhianna thought detachedly, with the Seymours and Penvarnons on one side of the private bar, and Clan Rawlins on the other. It was to be hoped that the knives in the dining room weren't that sharp, or there could be mayhem.

She was keeping strictly to the edge of the room, away from the small charmed circle of well-wishers where Carrie stood, her arm through Simon's.

She hadn't looked at him, or he at her, while they'd murmured their conventional and meaningless greetings to each other.

Would there ever come a time when she could look at him and see simply Carrie's husband? Maybe one day—once time and distance had done their work. Or that was all she could hope.

She knew, of course, the exact moment that Diaz arrived, and for a blinding instant she wished with real savagery that she could turn back the clock and wipe out the past months with their burden of lies, secrets and shame.

That she could turn and see him standing in the doorway and be free to walk to him, smiling, and say in her turn, 'Diaz—it's been a long time.' And offer him her hand, or even her cheek. That she could see the silver eyes warm with surprise—and something more…

That it could be a beginning, and not an end.

Except that it was too late for that. Too much had happened.

Now, she could hear the buzz as he worked his way round the room. Knew when he'd paused to shake hands and hold a brief conversation with another guest, even as she herself listened politely to the elderly woman beside her. As she responded gracefully to what the other was saying about her favourite characters in *Castle Pride*, with Lady Ariadne very clearly not included among them.

Felt her heart quicken and her mouth dry as he reached her.

'Rhianna,' he said silkily. 'You take my breath away. This evening will be a real privilege.'

She watched him looking at her, frankly assimilating the way her dress clung to her breasts and hips. How the sash reduced her waist to a handspan.

'Allow me to return the compliment,' she returned crisply. One swift glance had been enough to inform her of his immaculately cut dark suit, the crisp whiteness of his shirt, and the sombre silk magnificence of his crimson tie.

'I'm sorry I'm a little late. I had some business to attend to.' He paused. 'Is there anyone else you wish to speak to? Or may I steal you away now?'

Rhianna shrugged. 'We're having a duty dinner,' she said. 'It's hardly an elopement.'

'Then let's go,' he said. 'Before we're arrested and charged with criminal damage to a tiara. I saw Mrs Rawlins bristle as I walked in.' He took her hand and smiled at her companion. 'Will you excuse us?'

She looked arch. 'With pleasure,' she said. 'And may I say you make a very handsome couple?'

No, Rhianna wanted to scream. You may say nothing of the kind. In fact you aren't even allowed to think it. And if the ground would open and swallow me, I'd regard it as a blessing.

But the floor remained in its usual robust state as she walked across it to the door, hand in hand with Diaz Penvarnon, acutely aware of the curious stares and whispers following them.

In the foyer, she detached herself coolly and firmly. 'We really don't have to do this,' she said. 'We can part company here and now and no one will be any the wiser.'

'So what's your alternative?' Diaz asked softly. 'Mourning your loss over a solitary scampi and chips at the White Hart?' He shook his head. 'No way, Rhianna. I asked you to have dinner with me, and the invitation stands—however distasteful you may find it.'

She hesitated, then reluctantly followed him out of the hotel. She glanced around her. 'I don't see the Jeep.'

'It was needed elsewhere,' he said. 'Besides, it's a beautiful evening. I thought we'd walk. Will your shoes allow that?'

'Of course.' But where on earth could they be going? she asked herself in bewilderment. The hotel, the pub, Rollo's Café, plus the fish and chip shop in Quay Street constituted Polkernick's entire claim to gourmet fame, as far as she was aware.

It was only when they reached the harbour and she looked out across the water to the sleek, beautiful motor yacht, riding there at anchor, dwarfing everything around it, that she realised.

'Your boat?' Her voice rose as she turned to him. 'You expect me to have dinner on your boat?'

'Why, yes.' He smiled at her. 'It's like a millpond out there, Rhianna. You can't be that poor a sailor. And I have an excellent chef, so what's the problem?'

You are, she thought, and I am. I'd prefer not to be quite so alone with you, but to have other people at other tables around us. And I can't walk on water if I need a quick exit.

As she hesitated, he added, 'It was either *Windhover* or the Boathouse at Garzion again, and I felt that might be a trip too far down memory lane for both of us.'

'How right you were.' Her own smile was forced. 'Well—if this is the deal, let's go. After all, we don't want to keep your chef waiting.'

And felt her heartbeat quicken as she went with him.

CHAPTER FIVE

AT THE harbour wall, she was forced to take his hand again to negotiate the slippery steps down to the waiting dinghy, where a grizzled man helped her aboard, his teeth flashing in a smile that managed to be admiring and respectful at the same time.

'This is Juan,' Diaz said casually. 'He helps me with the boat. His brother Enrique does the cooking.'

An efficient outboard motor propelled them across the calm water to the side of the yacht and a small platform at the foot of a broad steel ladder, leading to the upper deck, where Enrique, dressed in dark trousers and a white coat, waited deferentially to show her to the companionway leading down to the saloon.

Carrie's 'floating hotel suite' didn't even begin to cover it, she thought, looking round her in astonishment at the elegant pale tweed sofas grouped round a large square table, with drawers and cupboards beneath it.

Behind the seating area was a dining table, large enough to seat eight people, but tonight set only for two. And beyond that, judging by the delectable smells, was the galley.

'A drink?' Diaz suggested as Enrique disappeared, presumably to put the finishing touches to their meal. 'I can offer you fresh orange juice, if you're still swearing off alcohol.'

She noticed decanters and glasses waiting on a side table, and said lightly, 'If you can promise that Juan will be there to save me if I fall overboard, then I'll have sherry, please, as dry as possible.'

'If memory serves, you're probably a better swimmer than he

is,' Diaz observed drily. 'But let's say I guarantee that drowning won't be an option.' He handed her the sherry and raised his own glass. '*Salud!*'

She echoed the toast a little shyly, and sipped. She looked at him, her eyes widening. 'That's superb.'

'I'm glad you approve. You're permitted to sit down.'

She complied, and he took the seat opposite. 'I'm still trying to take it all in,' she said frankly. 'It's just amazing. And it—she—really is brand-new.'

'Just out of her trials,' he agreed. 'She's the new version of my previous boat and rather more powerful, giving me a greater range.'

'I—I didn't realise you were interested in boats.'

'How could you?' he said. 'You went off to London when you were eighteen, shaking the Cornish dust off your shoes. I'm sure you haven't forgotten.'

'No.' She didn't look at him, aware that her throat was tightening.

'And we haven't seen a great deal of each other since that time,' he went on slowly. 'Or not until the last few months when we—met again. And once we had met there were always other things to talk about. We never really got around to my leisure interests, if you remember.'

She stared down at her glass. 'I'm hardly likely to forget.'

'Yes,' he said. 'I think that at least is true, if not the whole truth.' He gave a harsh laugh. 'The curse of a good memory.' He paused. 'So, tell me something, Rhianna. Why, in spite of everything, did you come to this bloody wedding?'

'Because I couldn't think of a convincing reason to stay away,' she said. 'I could hardly tell Carrie that I was being pressured by you. She might have asked you for an explanation, and imagine how embarrassing that would have been. What price the whole truth then?' She paused. 'Anyway, I needed to say goodbye.'

The firm mouth curled.

'To Carrie.' She gave him a defiant look. 'And to all the rest of it. Everything. Cutting the last links for good. You should find that reassuring.'

He contemplated the pale liquid in his glass. 'Very little about you reassures me, Rhianna.' He leaned back against the cushions. 'Tell me, have you seen any more of your reporter friend, or hasn't he managed to track you down yet?'

'You clearly have a very broad view of friendship,' she said shortly. 'But the gentleman concerned—another loose term— seems to have returned to the hole he crawled out of. I only hope he stays there.'

'Amen to that.' He was watching her, the silver eyes sombrely intent. 'I did wonder, of course, if you were planning to hand him the scoop of his career. "Lady Ariadne claims another victim in best friend's nightmare." "Bridegroom flees with TV star." Or something of the kind.'

Her fingers tightened round the stem of her glass. 'What a vivid imagination you have,' she remarked. 'And you seem to have captured the gutter jargon perfectly. Maybe you missed your vocation.'

'Then I'm glad at least one of us has fulfilled his or her potential,' he said. 'Tell me something. Did the television company realise at once it was typecasting, or did you actually have to sleep with someone in order to play Ariadne?'

Oh, God. *Oh, God...*

Pain and outrage, which she could not afford to let him see, clawed at her. She leaned back in her turn, smiling at him with a fair bid for insouciance.

'Believe me, you really don't want to know,' she drawled. 'But I can swear that the casting couch was never as comfortable as this one. Does that satisfy your curiosity?'

She saw a sudden flare of colour along the high cheekbones, a glint in his eyes that might have been anger, or something less easy to define, and felt a stab of bitter triumph.

But when he spoke his voice was even. 'That,' he said, 'is something that *you* really don't want to know. And I think Enrique is ready to serve dinner.'

She would have given a great deal to damn him and his dinner to hell and leave. But that, of course, was impossible. She was virtually trapped there.

And if she insisted on being put ashore immediately he

would know that she was not as unaffected by his jibes as she wished to appear.

Besides, Sod's Law was kicking in, reminding her that she'd eaten very little for the past twenty-four hours, and her usual appetite was being forcibly awoken by the enticing aromas of Enrique's cooking.

She rose in silence and followed him to the dining area, realising with chagrin that she would not be facing him from the opposite end of the long table, but had been seated instead at his right-hand side. Almost close enough to touch.

An altogether too cosy, too intimate placing, but presumably done according to his instructions.

But, whatever game Diaz Penvarnon was playing, she would be a match for him, she told herself with determination.

He held the chair for her courteously, and she sank on to it with a murmured word of thanks, sending him a glancing smile.

This was how to play it, she thought, however much it might hurt. So for the next hour or so Diaz would find himself dining with none other than Lady Ariadne—'the Tart without a Heart', as one tabloid had christened her. Television's favourite Bitch Queen, never more dangerous or desirable than when she was planning something.

She would eat and drink whatever she was offered. She would keep up her side of any conversation and be charming. She might even flirt a little, letting her eyes under the long fringe of lashes offer him all kinds of possibilities. Knowing she was unreachable. Untouchable.

And once the meal was over she would yawn prettily, excuse herself, then leave.

Because first thing in the morning, wedding or no wedding, she would be inventing some dire emergency that required her elsewhere immediately, and catching the next available train out.

Which, she told herself, would finally be the end of it. She could not afford to look back. Or to hope. Not again. Not ever.

Although London wouldn't necessarily be her first destination of choice, she thought wearily. It was hardly a sanctuary for her these days. Even now there were going to be issues to be dealt with before she could attempt to get her life back on track.

And there was also Daisy to consider. Daisy, her friend, whose husband had left her, and who would be shocked and frightened, needing all the comfort and support Rhianna could give her.

But at least, she told herself, that would force her to put the sorrow of her own rejection, her own loneliness and fear, to the back of her mind until she was somehow strong enough to deal with them. Whenever that might be.

She stifled a sigh as she shook out her linen table napkin.

In this whole, reeling, unhappy mess, her only certainty was that it would not be soon. That it would take every scrap of courage she possessed even to survive.

And that the campaign was starting here and now, at this table, with this man.

If the circumstances had been different, she would have openly revelled in the food a beaming Enrique brought to them.

The first course was an array of *tapas*, individual little dishes of spicy sausage, olives, prawns, anchovies and marinated peppers. This was followed by a fillet of lamb, pink and tender, served with garlicky roasted vegetables, and the meal concluded with almond creams, all of it served with a flavoursome Rioja.

It was a delicious and leisurely performance, with Diaz suddenly transformed into the perfect host, and Rhianna found, to her own surprise, that she was perceptibly relaxing her guard as the evening went on. Which could be dangerous.

'Goodness,' she said, half-laughing at one point. 'All this, plus Juan and Enrique too. Is this some reversion to your Spanish ancestry?'

He shrugged. 'It's pointless to deny it exists, and just occasionally over the generations it comes roaring back.' He drank some wine. 'We were all pirates at the time of the first Elizabeth, the Spanish and the English alike,' he went on reflectively. 'All raiders and looters, feathering our nests in the name of patriotism. Taking what we wanted when we saw it, and to hell with the consequences. And my many times great-grandfather was certainly no different. Before his ship went down Jorge might even have been the man lighting the torch that fired Penzance. *Quien sabe?* Who knows?'

'And then he met Tamsin and married her,' Rhianna said quietly.

'Met her and seduced her,' he corrected. 'A fairly high-risk initiative in those days. Her father might as easily have slit his throat as said, "Bless you, my children. The wedding's on Thursday."'

'But it worked out well,' she persisted. 'He stayed on in an enemy country so he must have loved her.'

'Perhaps,' he said. 'But don't forget she was an heiress, and he was then a younger son with his way to make in the world. A few lies about his origins, and a crash course in English may not have seemed too high a price at the time. His own good fortune came later.'

'What a cynical point of view,' Rhianna said lightly. 'I prefer the romantic version.'

His mouth hardened. 'With true love triumphant, no doubt? I can see why that would appeal. Unfortunately real life rarely supplies neat endings.'

'So I've discovered.' Her smile was brief and taut. She needed to change the subject, and quickly. She looked down at her empty plate. 'But Enrique is a gem. Surely he can't be content to hang around on your boat simply waiting for you to show up? He must get bored while you're in South America, or doing your global thing. Isn't he ever tempted to spread his wings—open his own restaurant, perhaps?'

'He's never said so.' Diaz refilled their glasses. 'Why not ask him?'

She flushed. 'Don't be absurd. After all, it's none of my business.'

'I think he'd be flattered,' he said. 'But probably not tempted. He likes his life, and so does Juan. Maybe they've found the recipe for happiness, and want to hang on to it.'

'While for the rest of us the search goes on.' She glanced at her watch. 'Heavens, it's nearly midnight. I should be getting back.'

Diaz also consulted the time, brows lifting. 'Why? The party at the hotel surely won't be over yet.'

'Indeed it will,' she said briskly. 'Carrie has to be home by twelve. You've forgotten the old superstition about the groom not seeing his bride on the wedding day until they meet in church.'

'In all the other excitement it must have slipped my mind. Nor am I particularly superstitious, except when it comes to mines.' He paused. 'I can't persuade you to have coffee, then?'

'Thank you, but not this late,' she said. 'It would keep me awake.'

As if there's any chance of sleeping, anyway...

'And naturally you wish to be at your brightest and best tomorrow,' Diaz commented silkily. He paused. 'However, to use a coy euphemism, would you like to freshen up before you go? If so, I'll get Enrique to show you to one of the staterooms.'

'Yes,' she said, reaching for her purse. 'That would be—most kind.'

'De nada,' he said. 'Even pirates can have their moments.'

At the door she hesitated, looking back at him for a moment, at ease in his chair, studying the rich colour of the wine in his glass. Knowing that this was probably the last time she would ever see him and that this was the image she would take away with her, imprinted on her mind—the dark, intelligent face, with its high cheekbones and those amazing long-lashed eyes, and the lean, long-legged muscular body.

Another companionway led down to the sleeping accommodation. The stateroom that Enrique showed her with obvious pride made her jaw drop. The fitted wardrobes and dressing table were made of some pale, expensive wood, while the bed, the widest she'd ever seen, was made up with cream linen, a bedspread in vibrant terracotta folded across its foot. The same colour was echoed among the piled-up pillows, and a small sofa, similarly upholstered, stood against one wall.

Or perhaps they were called bulkheads, she thought. She couldn't remember, and it didn't really matter anyway. It wasn't something she'd ever need to know.

The adjoining bathroom was all gleaming white and azure, with a walk-in power shower, a vanitory unit with twin basins, and a bidet as well as a loo.

'The *señorita* approves?' Enrique asked, pointing out the towels stacked on a corner shelf, and satisfying himself that there was soap in the dish between the basins. 'If there is anything else you require, tell me, *por favor*,' he added, turning to leave. 'There is a bell.'

Thoughtful, Rhianna decided with faint amusement, as she waited to hear the outer door close softly. But unnecessary.

Probably Enrique was more accustomed to women guests who spent longer than just one evening on board with his boss, and who shared far more than dinner.

Whereas I, she thought, swallowing, have to go and put the remains of my life back together.

She dried her hands, and dropped the used towel into the laundry basket, then ran a comb through her hair, wondering whether to renew her lipstick and deciding against it.

As she was doing so, she noticed the toiletries grouped together on the tiled top by the mirror, realising they were all her favourite brands—from the moisturiser to the perfumed body lotion, and even the shampoo.

Odd, she thought, and walked back into the other room, where she checked, her eyes narrowing. Because something else had suddenly appeared on the bed. A woman's nightgown, exquisitely fanned out. *Her nightgown...*

Rhianna took a deep breath, telling herself that it was some weird trick of her imagination, or more likely that she'd had too much of that wonderful Rioja.

At the same time, her instinct told her that she was fooling herself. She spun round and went back into the bathroom to check out the toiletries, her stomach muscles clenching as she saw that they'd all been used before, and that the pretty striped bag which had contained them when she left London was now in a cupboard under the basin.

My things, she thought desperately. Here—on his boat.

A glance in the stateroom's fitted cupboards confirmed her worst fears. All the clothing she'd brought to Penvarnon House was there, neatly hung away, or folded in the drawers, while her travel bag and dress carrier were tucked away at the back of a wardrobe. Her handbag was there too, but, she realised, biting her lip, minus her wallet and passport.

And at that moment she became aware of something else— the steady throb of a powerful engine. And she knew, with horror, that *Windhover* was moving. That they'd sailed.

She almost flung herself at the stateroom door, twisting the handle one way then another, tugging it, dragging at it breathlessly, while swearing softly but comprehensively. Refusing to believe that it wasn't going to open, in spite of her best efforts, because it wasn't just stuck in some embarrassing way—but actually locked.

Telling herself that this wasn't—couldn't be happening. Not to her.

He'd implied that he was descended from a Spanish pirate, but this was the twenty-first century, for God's sake, not the sixteenth, and there were strict laws against hijacking on the high seas.

If Polkernick Harbour actually qualified as any kind of high sea, she thought, quelling the bubble of hysteria rising inside her.

She wanted to beat on the closed door with her fists, screaming to be let out, but a small, icy voice in her brain said this was exactly the reaction he'd expect and would allow for. Therefore it would get her nowhere.

She stepped back and considered as she strove for control. For an element of calm.

Enrique had clearly been busy while her back was turned. It wasn't just her nightgown that had been left ready for her. Mineral water and a glass had appeared on one of the shelves fitted to the bedhead, together with a plate of cinnamon biscuits.

Everything for the discerning prisoner, she thought grimly.

Including the aforementioned bell. Which she rang.

And which was answered with admirable promptness by Diaz himself. He'd discarded his jacket and removed his tie, leaving his shirt open at his tanned throat.

Rhianna faced him from the sofa, legs elegantly crossed, hands folded in her lap to hide the fact they were shaking.

Her brows lifted. 'Enrique's busy, trying on his jailer's costume, I suppose?'

'I thought you might be throwing things.' He closed the door behind him and leaned against it. 'And decided I'd rather they hit me.'

'You're all heart,' she said shortly. She paused. 'Just what do you think you're doing?'

'Taking you for a short but romantic cruise,' he said. 'At least I hope it will be romantic. However, the Bay of Biscay may rule against that.'

'I'm on the side of the Bay of Biscay.' She lifted her chin. 'Diaz, you're being ridiculous. You can't behave like this.'

'And just who is going to stop me?' His voice held faint amusement.

'Your own common sense, I hope,' she said coldly. 'We're both supposed to be attending a wedding tomorrow—your cousin, my oldest friend. You think our absence won't be noted? That people won't ask questions and start looking for us?'

'They won't have to,' he said. 'The letter I left for Carrie earlier when I was collecting your stuff from the house makes the situation perfectly clear.'

Her heartbeat seemed to be rattling against her ribcage. 'Then maybe you could offer me equal clarification. If it's not too much trouble.'

'Not at all.' He settled himself more comfortably against the door, hands in his pockets. 'I told her that we'd got together in London earlier this year, but things had gone wrong between us.' He paused. 'I didn't specify what, or how, but I said I felt I had a real chance to put things right if you and I could just be alone together for a while to work things out.

'I mentioned that I knew that you planned to leave straight after the wedding, and once you'd gone any opportunity to get you to myself would probably be blown too, and I couldn't risk it. So I was extending our dinner date into a trip on *Windhover* for a few days. A kind of advance honeymoon. I thought that was the kind of excuse that might appeal, as she's about to embark on a honeymoon of her own.'

He added unsmilingly, 'I also asked her to forgive us both, and wish us luck.'

She said huskily, 'You actually believe that anyone will be deceived by such nonsense? By that—tissue of lies?'

He shrugged. 'Why not? Admittedly my explanation may not go down well in some quarters, and Carrie will indeed be disappointed, but in this case I feel the end justifies the means.'

'But I don't agree,' she said. 'So I'd be glad if you'd turn this floating prison right around and take me back to Polkernick.'

'Not a chance, sweetheart,' he said. 'You're coming with me. You might not be my companion of choice, you understand, but—hey—the time will soon pass. And when we eventually put in somewhere, you'll find yourself on a flight back to London before you know it.'

'Kidnap is a crime,' she said. 'People end up in jail for things like this.'

'For "kidnap" substitute "brief idyllic interlude for two people who fancy each other like crazy".' His smile was cold. 'Quite apart from the note, I think most of the evidence is on my side. Mrs Henderson was delighted to collaborate in my "surprise" and pack your things for Juan to collect after you'd left for the hotel. Everyone saw us leave the party in perfect amity, and knew we were having dinner together. There was no kicking and screaming at the harbour. There were people around who can verify that you came on board without coercion.'

'But that's not how I've stayed,' she said tautly. 'You had me locked in.'

'Did I?' he countered. 'Or have we just experienced some teething troubles with an ill-fitting door, perhaps?'

'No doubt that will be confirmed by Enrique,' she said bitterly. 'But it makes no difference. Because now I want to leave.' She swallowed. 'I don't even have to go back to Polkernick, if that's inconvenient. There are loads of harbours along the coast. You could simply drop me ashore at one of them, and be rid of me. I—I promise I'll make no official complaint.'

'A selfless thought,' he returned. 'And a real temptation. But no chance, my pet. We're sailing off into tomorrow's sunrise. Together.'

'But why are you doing this?' Her voice was a strained whisper. 'Why? I don't understand.'

Diaz straightened, coming away from the door and walking across to her. Standing over her so that in spite of herself she shrank back against the cushions.

His voice bit. 'To make sure that Carrie's wedding, however

ill-advised I may think it, goes ahead, unhindered and unhampered by any dramatic revelations from you, darling.'

His eyes were hard. 'You see, Rhianna, I just don't think you can be trusted. I think you spell trouble in every line of that delectable body that you use to such effect. But what finally tipped the scales against you was when I caught you parading yourself in front of the mirror yesterday—taking advantage of Carrie's momentary absence to see how her wedding dress and veil would look if you were wearing them instead of her.'

Rhianna felt the colour drain from her face. 'So it was you,' she said. 'I thought I heard someone.'

His mouth curled. 'Unfortunately for you—yes. I could hardly believe what I was seeing. Dear God, you'd only been in the house five minutes and already you were pretending to be the bride. Imagining yourself taking her place. And who could guarantee you might be not be tempted to turn your pathetic little fantasy into reality?'

She said hoarsely, 'Diaz—you have to let me explain…'

'Not necessary,' he said. 'You see, I came back a little later to tell you—warn you that I'd seen you—and tell you for the last time to go. Only I discovered that you were otherwise engaged, talking to bloody Simon.'

She said thickly, 'And you listened?'

'Wild horses wouldn't have dragged me away,' he returned harshly. 'It was—most revealing. Everything finally made a kind of sick sense.'

He looked at her with contempt. 'I don't know if being pregnant by the bridegroom is the kind of "just impediment" the Church was thinking of when it wrote the marriage service, but I sure as hell wasn't planning to find out. I couldn't risk you staging some hysterical last-minute confession scene, Rhianna, some touching plea for your unborn child. So I decided it would be better if you were removed—out of harm's way. And, ironically, Simon's ghastly mother supplied me with the means.'

'How fortunate for you,' she said hoarsely. 'And if she hadn't?'

'I'd have found some other way.' He gave her a cynical look. 'And you won't be gone for too long,' he added. 'Not enough to jeopardise your abortion plans anyway. I presume there's an appointment already booked?'

'Yes,' she said. It was difficult to speak evenly. 'As it happens, there is.'

'Good,' he said. 'Always best to keep things neat and tidy. Although even if Simon had been free to marry you I can't imagine you wanting to have the child,' he went on. 'After all, nothing must impede your precious career, and a pregnant Lady Ariadne would never do.'

'Totally out of character, I agree.' She lifted her brows, fighting the pain that raked her. 'I didn't realise you were such a fan.'

'I'm not,' he said. 'I simply found it—instructive. To see what you've become.'

'I've become a highly paid professional actor,' she said stonily. 'I'm not ashamed of that. But my screen persona and my private life are leagues apart, whatever you may want to believe. And forget that garbage about the casting couch too. I don't go in for casual sex. As you would have found out, Mr Penvarnon, dinner is one thing, but I'd have to love a man before I slept with him.'

She saw his jaw muscles clench and braced herself for anger, but when he spoke his voice was cool.

'Then let me put your mind at rest,' he said. 'The term "advance honeymoon" was only a figure of speech. I wouldn't really want Simon Rawlins' leavings.'

'I'm sure,' she said. 'But I still have a problem. As you've already noticed, I'm pretty recognisable, and if we're seen together—in Spain, France, or anywhere else—the obvious conclusions will be drawn.'

'Maybe,' he said. 'But when we resume our totally separate lives they'll have to think again.'

'And I know what they'll think,' she said curtly. 'That I'm your discarded mistress. You talked about potential headlines earlier. Well, I can see these now: "Ariadne dumped." "Millionaire turns down TV's Sex Siren." I don't court bad publicity. I can't afford to. And I shouldn't think you want it either.'

She paused. 'Especially if people start digging around, unearthing old scandals. How long, do you think, before that nasty little man from the *Duchy Herald* is told gloatingly by someone that my mother was your father's mistress? That she betrayed a sick woman who trusted her, and destroyed her marriage, driving her into a nervous breakdown. Which is why Esther Penvarnon lives in widowed exile to this day—because it's too painful for her to return.'

She drew a harsh breath. 'Isn't that still the authorised version of what happened?'

'You, of course, have a different one.'

'I certainly have another perception of my mother. You never knew her.'

'No,' he said. 'And you never knew mine.'

'True. However, I'm sure she wouldn't want those stories rehashed either, or served up as background to your supposed involvement with me.'

'Indeed not,' he said. 'So I shall make damned sure that our "supposed involvement" remains our little secret, and I advise you most strongly to do the same. Unless you think I missed the vague threat in your last remark.'

He paused. 'I'm not planning to parade you through the streets of Barcelona, sweetheart, or sunbathe nude with you by a pool on the Côte d'Azur. The paparazzi can't board this boat, and this is where you'll stay—until the wedding's past and gone and the happy couple far away where you can't touch them.'

He sent her a grim smile as he turned to leave. At the door he hesitated, glancing back at her. 'In retrospect,' he said, 'wouldn't it have been better just to have taken my advice and stayed in London? Think it over, if by some mischance you can't sleep. Goodnight, Rhianna.'

'In retrospect,' she said, 'wouldn't it have been better, in fact, if you and I had never met? You think about that.'

The door closed behind him, and this time she heard the key turn in the lock. For a moment she sat motionless, then she drew a long quivering breath and bent forward, covering her face with her hands.

While in her head a voice whispered over and over again, What can I do? Oh, God, what I can I do? How can I bear this?

But she heard only silence in reply.

CHAPTER SIX

As a confrontation, she thought painfully, it had not gone too well. She might have had the last word, but the upper hand had eluded her completely.

What on earth had possessed her to rake up past history to throw at him? They both knew what had happened, and nothing could change that—a certainty she'd lived with during the whole five years since she'd first learned the truth.

The summer when her life had changed forever.

She'd had her eighteenth birthday, acknowledged as usual by a card from her aunt, and celebrated joyously by a night out in Falmouth with Carrie and some of the girls from school. Her final examinations had been over, and she'd been waiting for the results—although her grades hadn't really been all that important, she reflected unhappily, as Aunt Kezia had refused point-blank to allow her to apply for a university place, unlike Carrie, who'd been hoping to go to Oxford.

'It's time you went out to work, my girl,' Miss Trewint declared harshly. 'Started contributing to your upkeep.'

In the meantime, almost as soon as the school gates closed, she found Rhianna a job for the season at Rollo's Café. The hours were long, it was poorly paid, Mrs Rollo was a witch and by the time her board and lodging had been extracted Rhianna was left with little to show for each week's hard work.

And this, she supposed, was to be her future. Or some dead-end office job, using the computing and word processing course from school, bolstered by weekend and evening work during the summer.

The only bright spot on the horizon was the anticipation of Carrie's eighteenth birthday, which was going to be marked by a major party at Penvarnon House.

And for once Simon was expected to be there.

He'd pretty much faded out of the picture since he'd gone up to Cambridge two years ago. He still came to Polkernick sometimes in the summer, when his parents were there, but they were fleeting visits, and often he was accompanied by friends from university, his time occupied with them. Sometimes, too, the friends were female.

Instinct told Rhianna, suffering her own pangs, how much Carrie must be hurt by this, and by the fact that her regular letters to Simon had been answered so infrequently since he left for university.

'He's frantically busy, of course,' she'd said once, her clear eyes faintly shadowed. 'With work and all the other stuff he's involved in. Because it's a different world. Everyone says so. Three years of complete whirl.' She'd paused. 'Besides, everything changes. We all move on, and I shall too.'

But Rhianna wasn't convinced. And her own dream image of Simon the Golden wasn't quite as perfect as it had been once, its gold just a little tarnished.

She wondered if he was bringing anyone to Carrie's party, and hoped devoutly that he wasn't.

She'd been invited, although naturally she wouldn't be attending the dinner that would precede the dancing. Judging by Carrie's obvious embarrassment, it was clear her mother had vetoed any such idea.

Carrie had the world's loveliest dress, in aquamarine chiffon, and Rhianna couldn't hope to emulate that. However, a charity shop in Truro had yielded a simple black slip of a dress in a silky fabric, cut on the bias with shoestring straps, nearly new, in her size and affordable. They'd even found her a pair of high-heeled sandals to match—which, the helper had confided, had proved too narrow-fitting for most of their customers.

'Might have been made for you, my handsome,' she'd said cheerfully, as she'd wrapped them.

And they did look good, Rhianna thought as she gave herself a last critical once-over before the party. She was just turning from the mirror when her door opened abruptly and her aunt marched in.

'They're going to be a waitress short at the dinner tonight,' she said, her eyes sweeping scornfully over Rhianna's slim figure. 'One of the girls is sick, so I told Mrs Seymour you'd take her place.'

Rhianna gasped helplessly. 'But I can't do that. Carrie's invited me to the dancing as a guest,' she protested. 'You know that. And I bought this dress specially.'

'Yes, and a rare waste of money too. Good job you have it to burn.' Miss Trewint tossed the dark button-through dress and frilled white apron she had over her arm onto Rhianna's bed. 'Well, you won't be parading yourself like a trollop tonight, madam. So get changed and over to the house, and sharp about it. People will be arriving. And tie your hair back.'

The door banged behind her. Throat tight, eyes burning, Rhianna hung the black dress back in the wardrobe and put on the navy uniform. It was a size too big, but she tied the apron more tightly round her waist to give it more shape. She dragged her hair back from her face and plaited it quickly, her fingers shaking, then changed her sandals for the low-heeled pair she wore at the café.

The hired help, she thought bitterly, and looking just as drab as Aunt Kezia could have wished.

Carrie met her with a look of utter consternation. 'I don't believe this,' she said furiously. 'Your aunt—my mother—what the hell are they playing at?'

'Teaching me my place, I think.' Rhianna gave her a swift hug. 'Don't worry about it. We can exchange above and below stairs viewpoints afterwards.' She wanted to add, I really don't mind, but it wasn't true. She minded like blazes.

It was a very long evening. Rhianna carried round trays of drinks, platters of canapés, and later stood at the dinner, helping to serve the poached salmon and carve the turkey.

Mrs Seymour, she thought, surreptitiously easing her aching feet as she watched Moira's lavender-clad figure floating radiantly among the guests, is certainly getting her money's worth. That is if she actually intends to pay me.

One of the first people she'd seen had naturally been Simon. 'Good God.' He'd looked her up and down blankly, then started to grin. 'If it isn't the lovely Rhianna. Bloody hell, I didn't realise this was supposed to be fancy dress.'

The friend accompanying him had roared with laughter, his hot brown eyes assessing Rhianna in a way she didn't like. She'd cared for him even less when she spotted him later, adding the contents of his hip flask to the non-alcoholic punch.

But the next time she'd seen Simon he'd been dancing with Carrie, his lips close to her ear, whispering things that had her blushing, her face radiant with a delight she couldn't have concealed if she'd tried.

And she wasn't trying very hard, Rhianna thought ruefully. So much for moving on.

During the course of the evening she'd also seen Diaz Penvarnon arrive late. She'd assumed he wasn't coming at all. At the sight of him, she'd longed to fade back into the wall, but he hadn't appeared to notice her, so perhaps the waitress gear had made her temporarily invisible.

Although there was no reason why he should care if she was there as friend or servant, she reminded herself.

Whenever he visited Penvarnon House he always spoke to her, but as if, she thought sometimes, he was taking care to be pleasant. Yet, while there'd naturally never been any repeat of that wonderful birthday dinner, he'd invariably remembered to send her a card when the anniversary came round.

It was getting on for midnight when Simon approached her again. 'Going to dance with me?' he asked, bending towards her, his face flushed.

'For goodness' sake, Simon, I can't,' she muttered. 'I'm here to work, and Mrs Seymour's watching me.' She raised her voice a little. 'Is there something I can get you, sir?'

'Absolutely. Dance with me and I'll tell you.' He grinned at her.

'Simon,' she said. 'This isn't funny. Please go away.'

'Poor Cinderella,' he said. 'But they can't keep you slaving all night. You deserve some fun. And you can at least have some champagne to toast Carrie's birthday, like everyone else. She'd want that.' He paused. 'Tell you what—I'll get a bottle, and we'll meet you round by the stables in ten minutes. How would that be?'

She bit her lip. 'Well, OK. But I can only stay a few minutes.'

When he'd gone, Rhianna glanced round her. She probably wouldn't be missed at this stage, she thought. No one wanted any more food, at least not until the eggs and bacon were to be served very much later on. And Aunt Kezia's eagle eye was now superintending the clearing-up operation in the kitchen. She probably could slip out for a little while. And if she was spotted then she would have Carrie to defend her.

Apart from the moon, there was no light in the yard. It was cooler now, too, after the heat of the house, and Rhianna hugged herself, shivering a little.

She called softly, 'Carrie?'

'Over here.' Simon's voice reached her from one of the disused loose boxes.

He was standing just inside, leaning against the wall, a dark shape among the shadows. As her eyes adjusted Rhianna realised he was alone, his tie loosened, and that he was clasping an open bottle of champagne, which he held out to her.

'So,' he said, his voice slurring a little. 'Here we are at last. Let's party.'

'Where's Carrie?'

'Being the obedient daughter and perfect hostess.' He said it with a laugh that was almost a sneer. 'Where else?'

'Then I should get back to being the perfect waitress,' she said. 'I haven't got time to party—or not without Carrie, anyway.'

'She won't miss you. Come on, Rhianna, loosen up.' Putting down the bottle, he pushed himself away from the wall and came over to her. 'Neither of us is on the A list tonight, so we may as well drown our sorrows.'

Judging by the alcohol on his breath, Simon's troubles were already well submerged. She drew back. 'No, thank you.'

'Oh, come on, sweetheart. What's your problem?' He looked her up and down. 'Don't pretend you don't fancy me. You have done for years. I heard all about it from a girl at your school. Only I didn't feel like following it up—then. But things—and people—change with time.' He paused. 'Who'd have thought it, eh? From scrawny kid to hot totty in one blink of the eye.'

She was getting more uncomfortable by the second. 'Simon, I have to get back—really.' She turned towards the house. 'People will be wondering where I am.'

'But my need,' he said thickly, 'is much greater than theirs— believe me.' He grabbed her arm, pulling her towards him. 'So stay and be nice. You know you want to.'

Caught off balance, Rhianna found herself pinned against him so closely that his state of arousal became embarrassingly evident.

She tried to say, Stop this now—but her words were smothered by the heat of his mouth, and his hands were tugging at the buttons of her dress.

Then from behind them, a man's cool voice said, 'So there you are, Simon. Everyone's looking for you, particularly Carrie. Your friend Jimmy's drunk and behaving rather badly.'

And, to her horror, Rhianna realised that the voice belonged to Diaz Penvarnon. And that he was standing watching them from the doorway of the loose box, dark brows raised, and his eyes like steel.

Simon let her go as if he'd been stung, and swung round defensively. 'What am I supposed to do about it?'

'You brought him.' Diaz sounded bored. 'You deal with him. He can hardly stand up, let alone walk. And go now, please,' he added as Simon seemed prepared to argue. 'Sorry to upset your pleasant interlude, but Carrie's mother is getting upset.' He paused. 'And so is Carrie.'

Simon shrugged almost airily. 'You know how it is, man.' He glanced, grinning, at Rhianna. 'If the offer's on the table, you can hardly turn it down—especially when it comes so nicely packaged.'

He set off across the yard, walking none too steadily himself.

Dazed, Rhianna watched him go, his words beating in her brain. She thought, He's deliberately made it sound as if this was my idea. As if I came out here to be with him—wanting—*this*…

She turned to Diaz, saw the direction of his gaze, and, looking down, realised her dress was unfastened almost to the waist.

'Oh, God,' she said. Dry-mouthed, fingers shaking, she attempted to fumble the buttons back into their holes.

'A little late for modesty, wouldn't you say?' His voice reached her harshly.

'You don't have to watch,' she said. 'I have to get back to work.'

'No,' he said. 'You don't. You're finished for tonight. The only place you're going is home to bed.'

She said tautly, 'Is that an order—sir?'

'Yes,' he said. 'It is.' He paused. 'So what was this? An extra birthday present for Carrie? Having her heart broken? Because if she'd turned up here instead of me that's what would have happened.'

He shook his head. 'You of all people should know how she feels about Simon Rawlins, Rhianna. And, whatever I think of him, I know that falling in love with the right person isn't always a given—at any age. Maybe he's like a virus, and she'll recover eventually, but that time is clearly not yet. So keep your predatory little hands off her precious apple cart—and that's another order.'

His words seemed to pelt her like stones, making her quiver under the onslaught. Because what could she say in her own defence? *It wasn't like that.* How feeble and unconvincing was that?

Besides, when Simon had grabbed her she'd been too stunned to react immediately, so she hadn't even been fighting him off when Diaz had walked in.

Making herself decent was no longer a priority. All that mattered was getting out of there—away from him—away from the icy condemnation in his voice for which she had no answer that he would ever believe.

But as she went past him he caught her arm, halting her.

The silver eyes were sombre. 'Is this how you rate yourself— sex in an empty stable with another girl's man? You disappoint me.'

'And of course we can't have that.' Anger and bitterness were at war inside her, making her reckless. 'But, as it happens, things would never have gone that far.'

'You imagine *you* were the one in control of the situation?'

he asked derisively. 'Not from where I was sitting, sweetheart. And a last-minute change of heart doesn't always work with someone half-cut and looking for mischief. If I hadn't followed you there could have been trouble.'

She stiffened. 'How good of you to take such an interest in an employee's private affairs,' she said. 'But also quite unnecessary. I can take care of myself.'

He said slowly, 'Can you indeed?'

'Yes,' she said. 'Of course.' And tried not to think of Simon's fingers on her flesh. The pressure of his mouth.

Diaz swung her round, pushing her against the outside wall of the stable. He put one hand on the brickwork beside her and leaned towards her, his other hand cupping her chin, his thumb rhythmically stroking the delicate line of her jaw.

He said softly, 'Are you quite sure of that?'

She looked up into his eyes. They were pale as the moonlight itself, the irises very dark. They held an expression she had never encountered before—with anyone. Certainly not with Simon a few minutes ago, she thought, and realised she was frightened and excited at the same time.

He added, 'Prove it.' Then bent his head and put his mouth slowly and carefully on hers, caressing her lips lightly and sensuously.

It was not the frank lust she'd experienced just now. Nor was it passion. Or not yet, anyway. Even in her comparative innocence Rhianna recognised that.

He was simply asking a question. Testing her quite gently, but also inexorably. This time demanding an answer.

She'd been kissed before tonight, of course. Not often, it was true, and certainly not well. The school had thrown a leavers' party with a disco, and several of the lads had tried their luck during the slow dances. She'd accepted those minor advances with good-humoured resignation, if not pleasure. The boys hadn't been strangers, after all, and she hadn't wanted to make a fuss or hurt anyone's feelings. But she'd moved away as soon as the dance was over, making it tacitly plain there'd be no repetition.

But this—*this*—was wholly different. As his kiss deepened,

coaxing her lips to part for him, his hand was tracing the curve of her slender throat, lingering on the leap and flutter of her pulse, then moving down to her loosened dress to stroke the first delicate swell of her breast and linger there.

Her reaction was instant, shocking her with its intensity. Making her aware of explicit sensations—needs—never before imagined, let alone experienced. Enticing her with the scent—the taste of him.

She wanted, she thought as her brain reeled, to answer all his questions. To twine her arms round his neck and feel the warmth, the male hardness of him against her. To return the pressure of his lips and more. To feel his touch on her naked skin and show him she was ready to be a woman. His woman, if he so desired.

But it seemed he did not.

Instead he was lifting his head and stepping back, his expression guarded as he studied her.

He said quietly, 'I think you seriously over-estimate your resistance levels, Rhianna. Just be glad I don't take sweets from babies, or you'd be spending the night in my bed, not your own. Which is a seriously bad idea for a great many reasons.' He added almost harshly, 'Now, run along, and don't go looking for trouble with men. Because you'll surely find it.'

He turned and walked away, and she stayed where she was, leaning against the wall, her legs shaking too much to move.

And at that moment a light came on, illuminating the entire yard—including the tall figure of Diaz Penvarnon crossing to the rear entrance of the house.

Rhianna turned her head, startled, and saw the dark shape of her aunt standing at the window of the flat, looking down. She couldn't see her face, but instinct warned she'd gone from one kind of trouble straight to another.

Reluctantly she moved, walking slowly round the yard to the flat door and going in.

Kezia Trewint was waiting for her in the living room, her face set, her deep-set eyes burning with anger and scorn as she looked at the girl hesitating in the doorway.

'So,' she said. 'You've been with him. Another Carlow woman chasing after a Penvarnon man. Just as I knew you'd be all those years ago.'

Rhianna gasped. 'What—what do you mean?'

'I mean you—up against the stable wall with Mr Diaz. A slut—a dirty little tart—just like your mother before you.' She drew a hoarse breath. 'Didn't she bring enough shame on our family? And *him* of all men?'

'No,' Rhianna managed. 'It—it wasn't like that...'

Oh, God, she thought. This was an entirely different level of misunderstanding. This was terrible.

'You think you weren't seen sneaking off, and him following?' Miss Trewint demanded derisively. 'That Mrs Seymour didn't go after him, and me with her? That we didn't see you with our own eyes? It's what the family have been expecting ever since you came here. Grace Carlow's daughter, and the living image of her. Made him wonder, I dare say, what Ben Penvarnon once had, and fancy a taste of the same.'

Her eyes rested on Rhianna's still unfastened buttons. Her sudden laugh was vicious, grating. 'But that's where it'll end. I promise you that. Because he's not like his father. Not that one. He won't be setting you up in some London flat and paying the bills in return for his pleasures. Now he's used you, he'll forget you. He can't do otherwise. Because *she* might find out, and he can't risk that.'

Rhianna stared at her. She felt very cold. 'I don't understand,' she said. 'What are you talking about. Who is *she*? And what are you saying about my mother?'

'She was Ben Penvarnon's mistress, bought and kept,' Miss Trewint flung at her. 'As everyone knows. And I was the one, God forgive me, who brought her into this house and put temptation in his way, flaunting herself in front of him.

'"Yes, Mr Penvarnon,"' she mimicked. '"No, Mr Penvarnon." "I think Mrs Esther's a little better today, Mr Penvarnon."' She drew a shuddering breath. 'Playing sweetness and concern for the sick woman she was supposed to be tending, and all the time she was running off to meet with her wedded husband in that hut on the beach or up on the moors. And you're proving yourself no better with his son.'

'That's a lie. And I don't believe what you're saying about my mother either.' Rhianna's chest was so tight it was difficult to breathe. 'She was in love with Daddy. You only had to see them together to know that.'

'What did she ever know about love?' Her aunt glared at her. 'All she knew was having her fun and wheedling all she could out of another woman's husband. And after he was dead, and there were no more pickings to be had, she had to do something. Find some other fool to keep her.'

Her mouth thinned. 'And you'll have to do the same, my lady. Don't think you're staying here after tonight's goings-on. Even if I was prepared to keep you, Mrs Seymour won't have it. Reckons you're an insult to her sister, and that Mr Diaz must have run mad to look twice at you with what he knows.'

'But nothing happened,' Rhianna protested desperately. 'Or not like you think, anyway,' she added. *But it could have done*, said a sly voice in her head. *He was the one who put a stop to it, not you, so no credit to you. And you can't even claim it was his fault—not this time.*

But I can't think about that, she told herself, wincing inwardly. I've got to forget those dark, urgent moments in his arms when nothing mattered but his mouth on mine and the touch of his hand on my skin.

'*A seriously bad idea for a great many reasons.*' That was what he'd said, and now she knew what he'd meant. Why he'd let her go. And why he'd do nothing to prevent her being sent away permanently. Not this time.

'Nor is it going to happen.' Miss Trewint's voice reached her grimly. 'So you can start packing your bags. I knew you were going to be a bad lot from the first, hanging round Mr Diaz whenever he came here. And there you were tonight, supposed to be working, but throwing yourself at any man who'd look at you.' She snorted. 'I should have turned you out two years ago, when you were sixteen, but for that headmistress of yours insisting you should finish your education—get more qualifications.' She shook her head. 'I was a fool to listen. But you'll make no more mischief here. You're going tomorrow, and good riddance too.'

But where am I to go? Rhianna wanted to ask. What can I do? I haven't earned enough to save anything, so what am I going to live on while I find work—somewhere to live? And although I never wanted to come here, and the last six years of my life haven't been that happy, at the same time they've been centred exclusively on this house. I've grown accustomed to it. I don't know anywhere else.

But she said none of those things aloud. She wouldn't argue, she thought. Nor would she beg.

I can take care of myself. Her own words, she thought. And if they'd been an empty boast a little while ago, she would have to live up to them now.

She was putting the last of her things in her only suitcase the next morning when Carrie put a cautious head round her bedroom door.

'It's all right,' she said. 'Your aunt's supervising the cleaning-up operation, stalking round like Medusa on a bad day.' She saw the open case and her eyes widened in distress. 'Oh, God, it's true. You're really leaving. I heard Mum and Dad rowing in the study when I came down, and apparently there was another huge row earlier, between Diaz and my mother, and he slammed out of the house and drove off somewhere. I thought he might simply be peeved about the state of the house,' she added glumly. 'Wine and food spilled all over the place, half the crockery and stuff abandoned on the lawn, and Simon, among others, getting totally wasted with his ghastly friend Jimmy, who was sick everywhere.' She groaned. 'Thank God I'll only be eighteen once. I couldn't go through all that again.'

She paused. 'But Mum was saying you had to go, and Dad was trying to reason with her, so what's happened?'

Rhianna bit her lip. 'Your cousin Diaz kissed me goodnight.' She tried to sound nonchalant. 'Your mother and my aunt both saw it, and as a consequence all hell has broken loose.'

Carrie gaped at her. 'But it wouldn't have meant anything,' she protested. 'Not from Diaz. He probably realised you were rightly miffed about the waitressing business and was just being kind again.' She sat on the edge of the bed. 'Face it, love,' she said gently. 'You're far too young for him. He dates the kind of women who go to first nights at the opera and have their photographs taken in the Royal Enclosure at Ascot. Mum knows that perfectly well.'

'Yes,' Rhianna said, trying to ignore the sudden bleak feeling in the pit of her stomach. 'But she also knows that my mother had a serious affair with your uncle Ben, and, however unlikely it may be, she doesn't want history to repeat itself.'

If she hadn't been so het-up she might have found the expression of blank shock on Carrie's face almost funny.

'I was going to say you must be joking,' she said at last. 'But clearly you're not. When did you find out about this?'

'Just before my sentence of banishment was pronounced last night.' Rhianna tried to speak lightly. 'In a way, it was a relief to know there is a reason for my having been the resident leper all these years. But it wasn't the most welcome news I've ever had either.' She looked at Carrie. 'You never knew—never guessed?'

The other shook her head. 'Never—cross my heart. But a lot of stuff finally makes sense,' she added soberly. 'Like being told I was too young to understand when I used to ask why Aunt Esther never came back here, even to visit.'

Her tone became brisker. 'But this isn't your fault, love. And Uncle Ben must have died at least four years before you were born, so there can't possibly be any connection there.'

She paused. 'Mind you, I remember Mrs Welling saying once that he'd always been a devil for the women—before and after he married Aunt Esther. So perhaps your mother wasn't really to blame either.' She pulled a face. 'Maybe it was one of those squire and village maiden things.'

'I don't think so.' Rhianna grimaced too. 'Apparently your aunt was ill and my mother was nursing her when it started. Which somehow makes it even worse—if it's true, of course.' She sighed. 'I can't believe anyone as warm and kind as my mother would have taken advantage of a sick woman by stealing her husband.'

She tucked her small make-up purse down the side of the case. 'What was wrong with Esther Penvarnon. Do you know?'

'Not really,' Carrie said, frowning. 'According to my mother she had a bad time when Diaz was born, and was never well afterwards. It might have been one of those virus things, like ME, because according to the Welling information service Aunt Esther spent a lot of time in a wheelchair.'

She frowned. 'Although I have to say Mrs W also claimed she could walk perfectly well if she wanted. She reckoned, and I quote, that my aunt should have "got up and got on with being Mr Penvarnon's missus," thus saving a heap of trouble all round.'

She paused. 'Especially for you. Talk about the sins of the mothers...' Her face acquired the stubborn look that Rhianna remembered from the first days of their friendship. 'However, you can't simply be thrown out on to the streets with nowhere to go.'

'But that isn't the case any longer. I *do* have a place to stay—back in London.' Rhianna forced a smile. 'Remember the Jessops, who looked after me after my mother died? Well, we've always stayed in touch, and over the years they've kept asking me to visit them—but I never could because Aunt Kezia said the fare was too expensive. Well, I phoned them this morning, and as soon as I tell them what train I'm catching they're going to meet me at Paddington. I can live with them again until I've found a job and got settled.'

'Well, thank God for that at least,' Carrie said roundly. 'But you've still been treated very badly by our family—Diaz included. If he wanted to kiss someone, why didn't he pick Janie Trevellin? After all, they were seeing each other when he was over last year, and Mother thought at one point they might even get engaged.'

She shrugged. 'Some hopes. One day he threw his stuff in the car, as usual, and went.' She gave a reluctant grin. 'According to Welling wisdom, Penvarnon men have always been restless. Never in one place, wanting to be somewhere else. "Hard to tie down, and impossible to keep tied after".'

Rhianna made herself speak evenly. 'Then maybe Janie Trevellin had a lucky escape.'

'I bet she doesn't think so.' Carrie watched Rhianna fasten her case. 'Look, are you quite sure about this? Perhaps things were said in the heat of the moment last night, and everyone will have calmed down by now?'

'Not my aunt,' Rhianna said briefly. 'Besides, I never planned to stay here for ever, so maybe being pushed into action now is actually a blessing in disguise.'

'Like the pigs currently flying over the roof,' Carrie retorted. 'You've got my mobile number haven't you. Let me know you're safe and sound, and keep in touch with all your new contact details. Oxford's much nearer London, so, fingers crossed, we can go on seeing each other quite easily.'

Rhianna took a deep breath. 'I'm sure you won't just be seeing me.'

'Well, no.' She flushed a little, her smile tender. 'Simon came over a little while ago, to grovel about Jimmy and a lot of other things besides. He said going to university, getting away from the family and finding his freedom, knocked him sideways for a while, but he's back on track now. And he wants to see me again—seriously this time.'

'Then last night clearly wasn't all bad.' Smiling was an effort, but Rhianna managed it. 'If he's truly the one, Carrie, go for it.' *But, please God, don't let it be true. Let her find someone else.*

'Don't worry,' Carrie assured her. 'I shall.' She paused again. 'How are you getting to the station? You can't possibly walk.'

'No choice. I certainly can't afford a taxi.'

'I shall take you,' Carrie said firmly. 'In Mother's car. And I shall ask her for the wages you're owed for last night, too.'

Rhianna stared into her shoulder bag on the pretext of checking its contents, aware that her face had reddened.

'Please don't,' she said constrictedly. 'I think that's best forgotten. Besides, I don't want anything from her. From anyone.'

But later, at the station, Carrie produced a roll of notes and handed them to her. 'For you,' she said. 'From my father, wishing you all the best.'

Rhianna stared at it in disbelief. 'But it's five hundred pounds,' she said. 'I couldn't possibly take it.'

'He says you have to.' Carrie looked awkward. 'It seems Uncle Ben left your mother some money in his will, but she refused to accept it. By comparison, this is a pittance, but Dad says it will make him feel much better, knowing that you're not penniless.'

'How lovely of him.' Rhianna felt perilously close to tears.

Francis Seymour was such a contrast, she thought, to her aunt, who'd said curtly, 'So you're off, then? No doubt you'll fall on your feet. Your sort always does.'

And Rhianna's brief but carefully prepared speech of thanks for the home she'd been given for the past six years had died in her throat.

And that, she thought now, was the last time I saw her.

The last time I believed I would see any of them.

And, oh, God, it would have been so much better that way.

CHAPTER SEVEN

HER face was wet again now, Rhianna realised, raising her head at last.

Stress, she told herself. A natural reaction to finding herself in this totally unnatural situation. Certainly not an appropriate time to start remembering the unhappiness of the past.

Especially when she should be concentrating all her energies strictly on the present—getting out of this mess.

And yet the past five years had certainly not been all bad. On the contrary. There'd been good things to treasure as well, she thought. The unfailing kindness of the Jessops, who'd treated her as if she'd never been away. Her continued friendship with Carrie, who'd secured her Oxford place with ease, and had only been sorry that Rhianna wasn't there with her.

And the wonderful Marika Fenton, the retired actress running drama classes at a local evening institute, who'd used jealously guarded contacts to get her star student into stage school, and chivvied the board of trustees into granting whatever bursaries might be going.

She'd written regularly to Aunt Kezia, but had never received a reply. Then her aunt had died very suddenly of a heart attack, before receiving the letter in which Rhianna told her she'd just won a leading role in a brand-new drama series called *Castle Pride*.

A clearly embarrassed communication from Francis Seymour had told her that Miss Trewint had given strict instructions that Rhianna was not to attend her funeral service or cremation, that her possessions should be sold and any money raised, together with her meagre savings, donated to the RSPCA.

Rhianna had accepted those harsh final wishes without protest.

The following day she'd begun to rehearse the role of Lady Ariadne. And the rest, as they said, was history.

She stood up, stretching. And history it had to remain. She had to deal with the here and now. Get through the pain of the next few days as efficiently as possible.

And to start with it seemed pointless to spend all night on this sofa when there was a perfectly good bed waiting, she told herself.

If she had to be miserable, then it might as well be in comfort.

So, having changed into her nightgown, performed her simple beauty routine, cleaned her teeth and brushed her hair, Rhianna slipped under the covers.

But sleep proved elusive. However much her mind might twist and turn, she could see no easy way out of this present disaster, she thought. Diaz had set a trap, and she'd walked blindly, insanely, into it.

And the old anodyne about things looking better in the morning didn't seem to apply in the current situation.

Unless she woke to find herself back in the primrose room, recovering from a particularly bad nightmare, she thought wryly. And how likely was that?

Eventually, however, the comfort of the mattress beneath her was too enticing, and the pillows too soft to resist, so that the next time she opened her eyes it was broad daylight.

She lay still for a moment. It's here, she thought. It's today. Carrie's marrying Simon and I'm not there. God help me, I'm in the middle of the ocean with Diaz Penvarnon. No bad dream. It's really happening.

There'd been some troubling moments in the night, she remembered painfully. Her mind had been invaded by disturbing images of weeping, unhappy girls, Carrie and Daisy among them, their faces blotched and swollen with emotion. And another, her expression haggard, the velvet dark of her pansy-brown eyes red-rimmed with tears.

That one most of all, she thought, moving restively.

Her reverie was interrupted by a tap on the door, and Enrique came in with a tray holding a cafetière, cup and saucer, and a cream jug.

'*Buenos dias, señorita,*' he greeted her respectfully, just as if he hadn't had to unlock her door to gain entry. 'It is fine today, with much sun, and the sea is calm. The *señor* hopes that you will join him for breakfast presently.'

A number of responses occurred to Rhianna, most of them occupying a position between fury and obscenity, but she reminded herself that Enrique was only obeying orders, and managed to confine herself to a quiet, 'Thank you.'

Alone again, she leaned back against her pillows and considered. A fine day, she thought. Wasn't there a saying about "Happy is the bride that the sun shines on"?

Oh, let it be true, she begged silently and passionately. Let Carrie's happiness be unclouded, and maybe that will justify this whole hideous business.

In a few hours' time the wedding would be over, anyway, and if there had ever been a time for intervention it was long past.

She could only hope and pray that Simon had been sincere when he'd claimed Carrie was the one he really wanted all along. But his straying could hardly be dismissed as a temporary aberration when it had left such misery in its wake.

Cape Town should be far enough away to give the pair of them a totally fresh start. No chance of embarrassing or agonised encounters in the street or at parties there. No startled recognition in theatre bars or restaurants.

London's a village, she thought. Sooner or later you bump into everyone. As she knew to her cost…

Stop thinking like that, she adjured herself fiercely. Today's going to be quite tricky enough, and you need to be on top of your game, so stop right now.

She turned determinedly to the coffee, which was hot, strong and aromatic, and she could almost feel it putting new life into her.

A shower helped too, even if the limitations of her wardrobe became all too apparent immediately afterwards.

With a mental shrug, she picked out the white cut-offs and the green and white striped shirt she worn on the beach at Penvarnon the previous day, and slid her feet into espadrilles.

She brushed her hair back from her face with unwonted severity, securing it at the nape of her neck with an elastic band which had begun its life round the folder containing her train ticket and seat reservation.

The return portion would now remain unused, of course, she thought. wondering ironically if the train company would deem being kidnapped as a valid excuse for a refund.

Another item, she told herself, to be added to the cost of my stupidity.

Biting her lip, she walked to the door. When she tried it this time, however, it opened easily, and, drawing a long, deep breath, she went out and up the companionway to join her captor.

She found Diaz on the sun deck, where a table and two folding chairs had been placed. He was casual, in shabby cream shorts and a faded dark red polo shirt, his eyes hidden behind sunglasses as he studied some very small item of hand-held technical gadgetry, which probably contained, she reflected, his bank statements, his address book and details of his business commitments for the next ten years.

And she thought how much she'd like to throw it overboard.

At her approach, however, he switched it off and rose courteously to his feet.

'Good morning,' he said. 'I hope you slept well.'

'No,' she said. 'But that was hardly likely—under the circumstances.'

His brows lifted quizzically. 'Because you've been under a certain amount of tension lately? Is that what you're saying?'

She thought of the anguished phone calls, the bitter outbursts, the threats of self-harm, and all those other truly sleepless nights, punctuated by harsh, heart-rending sobbing. All culminating in the final acknowledgement that Simon had gone, and all hope had gone with him.

She looked past him. 'You don't know the half of it.'

'One of those situations where ignorance is definitely bliss.'

His tone bit. 'But you're a really splendid actress, my sweet,' he went on, after a pause. 'Because when I came in to check on you, just after dawn, I'd have sworn you were flat out. I thought I even detected a little snore. How wrong can anyone be?'

She shrugged. 'I'd say the field was wide open.' She sat down, determined not to show her inner disturbance at the thought of him watching her sleeping, and unfolded her table napkin. 'But you seem to have insomnia problems too, if you were lurking around in the small hours.' She gave him a small, flat smile. 'Conscience troubling you, perhaps?'

'Not at all,' he said. 'These are busy waters. I had no wish for a moment's inattention to result in our being mown down by a tanker.'

The arrival of the attentive Enrique, with glasses of freshly squeezed orange juice and a basket of warm rolls, followed almost at once by scrambled eggs with chorizo and another large pot of coffee, saved her having to find a reply.

'I hope the sea air has given you an appetite,' Diaz remarked, offering her the pepper mill.

'I wouldn't know,' Rhianna said icily, aware, to her everlasting shame, that her mouth was watering in response to the aroma from her plate. 'Being shut up in that five-star cell you condemned me to, I didn't know it existed. After all, I could hardly open a window to check the ozone levels.'

'Well, your freedom has been now fully restored, and you can breathe again.' He indicated a powerful-looking pair of binoculars lying on the table beside him. 'Are you interested in birdwatching? It could be a good day for it, now we've left the sea mist off Brest behind us.'

'I'm afraid your plans for my shipboard entertainment are doomed,' she returned, doing her damnedest not to eat too fast, even though these were the best scrambled eggs she'd ever tasted. She added untruthfully, 'I really wouldn't know a canary from a robin.'

'I think Biscay goes in more for shearwaters and arctic terns,' he said. 'But maybe you prefer mammals. We can usually offer a selection of dolphins in good weather, or, if you're lucky, you might even spot a whale.'

'If I was lucky,' she said stonily, concealing a flash of delight, 'I wouldn't be here in the first place. And why would I want to see a whale anyway?'

'Because they're rare and beautiful creatures,' Diaz said quietly. 'I thought like might call to like.'

Rhianna looked down at her empty plate, her throat tightening as he paused.

'Besides,' he went on, 'you might get cast one day in another remake of *Moby Dick*, with the advantage of being already acquainted with the main character.'

'Unlikely,' she said, forbidding herself even a marginal smile. 'Female roles are pretty thin in that particular epic.'

'I'm sure they'd adapt it to accommodate you,' he said, pouring more coffee. 'A girl stowaway on the *Pequod* who slowly wins the heart of Captain Ahab and turns him from his revenge to joint ownership of a seafood restaurant on Nantucket.'

She shuddered. 'Oh, God, don't even suggest it. Someone might hear.'

'But if not that,' he said, 'there'll be other roles to play eventually.'

'I hope so,' Rhianna said slowly. 'I wouldn't like to think that Lady Ariadne would be all I'd be remembered for.' She bit her lip. 'But at the moment I'm not looking beyond the next series.'

'And what would have happened to that,' he enquired levelly, 'if Simon had asked you to marry him after all? If he'd wanted you to keep the baby? What price Lady Ariadne then?'

Be careful, said the voice in her head. *Be very careful. You can't give anything away.*

She shrugged again. 'That was never going to happen,' she said. 'I knew it. Simon certainly knew it. And we both made our choices long before you decided to interfere. Whatever you may have seen or heard, or think you know, the wedding was never in any danger from me.'

She sent him a cool smile. 'So now you'll have to live with the knowledge that it's all been a total waste of time. That you've carried me off for nothing, Mr Penvarnon.' She lifted her chin.

'Therefore, why don't you admit defeat, turn this expensive piece of equipment right around, and take me back to England?'

He pushed his chair back and rose. 'Because it's far too late for that, Rhianna,' he said softly. 'It always has been. And if you don't know that, sweetheart, then you're lying not just to me but to yourself as well.'

And he walked away, leaving her staring after him, her mouth suddenly dry and her pulses pounding.

In spite of the breeze, it was still hot enough for Rhianna to be thankful for the awning above the sun deck, where she lay on a cushioned lounger. But even in its shade her clothes were sticking to her.

I didn't bring a bikini on this trip, she thought wryly, because it never occurred to me I'd have time to sunbathe. Besides, I knew I could always borrow a costume from Carrie if I fancied a quick swim in between pre-wedding chores.

But maybe a bikini, or any kind of swimwear, would not be a good choice for these particular circumstances. Being fully dressed might not be comfortable, but it seemed altogether the safer option.

In view of his parting shot, she'd been half tempted to go to her stateroom and stay there, not venturing back on deck at all. But that might suggest she was disturbed by what he'd said, and she couldn't afford that. She had to appear indifferent, even relaxed, if that was possible.

So she'd simply collected her sunglasses, and the book she'd intended for the journey back to Paddington, and she was now struggling to lose herself in it. The reviews had been good, and it was by an author she liked, but the story was failing to hold her.

Real life seems to keep intruding, she told herself, endeavouring not to glance at the bridge, where Diaz, his shirt discarded, was seated at the controls, and thankful for the designer shades concealing the direction of her gaze.

What's wrong with me? she demanded silently. I've seen plenty of men in less than he's wearing. Come to that, I've seen him in far less too, only I was too young to appreciate it. Even if I've never been able to forget... But would the image of him emerging from the water like some dark sea god be the one she would take with her into the approaching wilderness?

Or would their encounters of a few months ago prove more potent in the end? Become the ones to be treasured?

Like the moment when she'd glanced across the crowded room at the sponsors' party and seen him there, unchanged and unmistakable after nearly five years, chatting to the Apex chairman and his wife.

She'd never really expected to see him again, so the shock of it had held her breathless, motionless for a moment, captive to all kinds of contradictory emotions. Then, obeying an imperative she'd barely understood but had known she might regret, she'd murmured an excuse to the group around her and begun to make her way towards him.

Halfway across the room, she had almost turned back.

I don't know what to say, she'd thought. Or even how I should behave. Surprised—that goes without saying. But should I be pleased to see him, or strictly casual? Just stopping for a quick word in passing on my way out to find a cab?

She had still been undecided when Sir John Blenkinsop had noticed her approach.

'Ah, delightful,' he said heartily. 'Diaz, you must allow me to introduce you to our star—the lovely girl who keeps the ratings for *Castle Pride* sky-high. Rhianna, my dear, this is Diaz Penvarnon, a valued client of Apex Insurance.'

There was an instant's silence, then Diaz said pleasantly, 'Actually, Sir John, Miss Carlow and I have already met. And delightful is certainly the word.' His eyes skimmed her, taking in the white brocade coat-dress, knee-length, its lapels designed to show a definite but discreet amount of cleavage. Then he took her nerveless hand in his and bent to kiss her cheek, his lips warm and firm as they brushed her face.

'Rhianna,' he said as he straightened. 'It's been a long time.'

Say something—anything…

'It has indeed. Too long.' Her numb lips managed to return his smile. 'I suppose this is one of your flying visits to the UK? Is it business or pleasure this time?'

'The usual mix,' he said. 'And my plans are fluid at the moment.' He paused. 'I've just come back from Polkernick.'

'Of course,' she said over-brightly, as guilt kicked in, reminding her of all the reasons she had to avoid him, and why she should have resisted this and every other temptation he represented to her. 'How—how is everyone?'

His grin was rueful. 'Wedding fever has risen to epidemic proportions,' he returned. 'If ever I tie the knot it's going to be at a register office very early in the morning. Guest list limited to two witnesses.'

'Oh, your bride will soon change your mind about that,' said Sir John. 'Women like these full-dress affairs, you know.'

Diaz said gently, 'Then I shall just have to persuade her.' He indicated the empty glass Rhianna was holding. 'May I get you another drink?'

'Yes, you look after her, my boy.' Sir John turned to his wife. 'Marjorie, my dear, I see Clement Jackson has arrived. He's bound to want a word, so shall we leave these two to catch up with each other?'

Rhianna stood, clawed by a mixture of excitement and uncertainty, as she waited for Diaz to return with the dry white wine she'd requested. I shouldn't be doing this, she whispered inwardly. I should be making an excuse and easing myself out. But I can't—I can't...

'Apparently Lord Byron said he woke up one morning and found himself famous,' Diaz remarked, as he handed her the glass. 'Was it like that for you?'

'Far from it,' she said. 'Although it's got trickier since. You become public property. People see me in their living rooms and think they know me.'

'How very optimistic of them,' Diaz said silkily. 'But it's good that you've prospered, Rhianna, after your precipitate exit from Polkernick. I was afraid the sight of me might put you to flight again.'

But I didn't jump—I was pushed...

Aloud, she said coolly, 'I think I'm a little more resilient these days.'

Am I? she thought. Am I—when the memory of you saying 'I don't take sweets from babies' still has the power to tear me apart? When just by standing here like this I know I could be setting up such trouble for myself?

She swallowed. 'I think Sir John's trying to attract your attention. He has someone he wants you to meet.' She sent him a brilliant smile. 'Enjoy your time in London.'

She walked away and didn't look back, her heart hammering painfully against her ribcage.

I've met him, she thought. I've spoken to him. And that's the end of it. There's no point in hoping, or wishing things could be different. Because that's never been possible.

She was halfway down the wide sweep of marble stairs that led to Apex Insurance's main foyer and the street, when she heard him speak her name.

She paused, her hand clenched painfully on the polished brass rail, then turned reluctantly.

He said evenly, 'Clearly we don't share the same definition of resilience, Rhianna, because here you are—running away again.'

'Not at all.' She lifted her chin. 'This evening was work, not social. So I've made my token appearance, kept the sponsors happy, and now I'm going home as planned. Job done.'

'Then change the plan,' he said softly. 'Have dinner with me instead.'

Her heart seemed to stop. 'Heavens,' she said lightly. 'What is this—some bridge-building exercise?'

'It's a man asking a beautiful woman to spend a couple of hours in his company,' Diaz returned. 'Do we really need to analyse it so closely or so soon? Why not simply see where it takes us.'

To disaster, she thought. There can be nothing else. So just utter a few polite words of regret and keep going. That's the wise—the sensible course. The only one possible.

She said, 'But you're clearly the guest of honour for Sir John. Won't he be upset if you disappear?'

'No,' he said. 'Nor surprised either. So will you be *my* guest of honour instead?'

And she heard herself say, unbelievably, 'Yes—I—I'd like that.'

Knowing, with mingled dread and anticipation, that she was speaking no more than the truth. That wisdom and common sense had counted for nothing the moment she'd seen him again. And that she was lost.

'I saw you as soon as I walked in tonight,' he said, as they faced each other across the candlelit table of the small Italian *trattoria*. 'There's only one head of hair like that in the entire universe. As soon as I'd finished being polite to my host I was going to come over to you.'

Rhianna put up a self-conscious hand. 'It's become almost a trademark,' she said, grimacing. 'I'm expected to wear it loose when I'm on show, like tonight. And my contract forbids me to cut it.'

'Of course,' he said. 'It would be a crime against humanity.' And his smile touched her like a caress.

She couldn't remember to this day what they'd eaten, although she was sure it had been delicious. She'd simply yielded herself completely to the luxury of being with him, just for that brief time.

Much later, outside, as he'd signalled to a cab, she'd said huskily, knowing she was a fool and worse than a fool, yet unwilling, in spite of herself, to let him go, 'Would you like some more coffee—a nightcap?'

And he said very quietly, 'Thank you. That would be—good.'

People were just coming out of the theatres, so the streets and pavements were crowded. As the taxi nosed its way along, Rhianna sat beside him in silence, hands clenched in her lap. Waiting and wondering.

She did not have to wait for long. And when Diaz took her in his arms she yielded instantly, her lips parting under the urgency of his kiss, her body pressed against his.

As she clung to him, she rejoiced secretly that her erstwhile lodger was no longer with her, and her flat was her own again. That she would be alone with him there. Then remembered that her precious privacy had come at a price.

She thought, If Diaz ever finds out about Simon...

Then, as his kiss deepened, she stopped thinking altogether,

her whole being possessed by the shock of desire. Because nothing mattered but the fact that she was with him—and the prospect, at last, of long-delayed surrender.

And she ignored the small warning voice in her mind that said, *This is so dangerous*, and allowed herself to be completely and passionately happy.

'*Señorita—señorita*—you come here quickly, please.' It was Juan, grinning with delight. 'Now, *señorita.*'

Startled back into the present, Rhianna got up from the lounger and followed him to the side of the boat, where Diaz was waiting.

'What's wrong?' She spoke curtly, her memories having left her unnerved and uncomfortable. But at least he was wearing his shirt again.

'Nothing at all.' He glanced at her with faint surprise. 'Look over there.'

Rhianna looked and gasped as a long silver body rose from the waves with a joyous twist, then disappeared again with a smack of its tail fin, to be followed by several more, their faces all set in that unmistakable half-moon smile as they jumped and soared.

'Oh, how wonderful.' She could not pretend sophisticated boredom when this amazing show was being performed as if for her exclusive benefit. She leaned on the rail, her face alight with pleasure, watching the dolphins cavort. 'Have you ever seen anything so beautiful?'

'Not often,' Diaz said quietly. 'Except in my dreams.' And she realised with shock that he was looking at her.

Her throat closed. *Oh, God, how can you say such things after everything that's happened? What do you want from me? Haven't I suffered enough?*

She stared at the gleaming, leaping bodies until they blurred, then with one last triumphant 'thwack' they were gone, and there was only the faint glimmer of them through the water as they sped away.

'The cabaret seems to be over,' Diaz commented. 'Conveniently, just in time for lunch.'

'More food?' Back in command of herself, she sent him a challenging look. 'I shall need a week at a health farm after this.'

'After this,' he said, 'the choice will be all yours.'

'Tell me something,' she said as they sat down. 'How much longer will it take to get where we're going?'

His brows rose. 'Is it so important to get somewhere?'

'Of course,' she said coldly. 'Because the faster we arrive, the sooner I can put this nonsense behind me and go home. Only we don't seem to be travelling very fast at all.'

She pointed to a large vessel in the distance that was steadily overhauling them. 'What's that, for instance?'

'The *Queen of Castile*,' Diaz said. 'Sailing between Plymouth and Santander.'

'Don't you find it faintly humiliating when you have all this power, purchased no doubt at vast expense, to be beaten for speed by a car ferry?'

'Not at all,' he said. 'This is a pleasure cruise, not a race. Anyway, I prefer to conserve fuel and have a comfortable passage.' He paused. 'But we should arrive at Puerto Caravejo in the early hours of tomorrow morning.'

'I've never heard of it,' she said shortly. 'Does it have an airport?'

'No,' he said. 'Just a pleasant marina, with some good restaurants. But you can fly to Gatwick from Oviedo. So, now that I've set your mind at rest, shall we eat?'

She wanted to say she wasn't hungry, because under the circumstances it should have been true, but once more Enrique's offerings proved irresistible.

The first course was a creamy vegetable risotto, studded with asparagus tips, tiny peas and young broad beans, and that was followed by grilled fish, served with crisp sauté potatoes, with fresh fruit for dessert.

Diaz consulted his watch. 'By my reckoning they'll be back from the church now,' he remarked. 'And just settling down to lunch in the marquee, with all its attendant rituals. So shall we drink a toast of our own?'

'To the happy couple?' Rhianna asked with irony. She shook her head. 'I don't think so.'

He was silent for a moment, and she saw his mouth harden. 'Naturally I can see that might not appeal,' he said, and picked up his glass of white wine. 'So let's just say—to matrimony.' And he drank.

'Forgive me,' she said, 'if I don't join in that either.'

He said with sudden harshness, 'He's gone, Rhianna. You've lost him. Accept it.'

Diaz paused. 'Coffee?'

'No, thank you.' Rhianna rose to her feet. 'I think I'll go below where it's cooler for a while.'

And where I don't have the nerve-racking disturbance of being in your company with all the attendant memories I can so well do without...

She added, 'Actually, I might start packing my things, ready for going ashore.'

'There's no great rush.' He sounded faintly amused. 'But— just as you wish.' He paused. 'Although I can recommend the old Spanish custom of *siesta*.'

She said unsmilingly, 'You're too kind. But I think I've already experienced enough old Spanish customs to last me a lifetime.'

Downstairs, the air-conditioning was as efficient as she'd hoped, and her stateroom was pleasantly dim too as someone— Enrique, she supposed—had closed the blinds.

Her refuge, she thought, as she sank down on the sofa. But, as she soon discovered, only a fragile sanctuary at best. Because, as she stared in front of her with eyes that saw nothing, she found there was no escape from her inner images of the past.

Or, she realised with anguish, their pain.

CHAPTER EIGHT

HER flat was on the first floor, and she and Diaz had run up the stairs, she remembered, laughing and breathless, hand in hand. Outside her door they'd paused to kiss again, all restraint gone. When they'd fallen apart, Rhianna's fingers had been shaking so much she'd hardly been able to fit the key in the lock, and Diaz, an arm clamped round her, his lips nuzzling her neck, had done it for her.

In the hallway they'd reached hungrily for each other again. His mouth pushing aside the loosened brocade lapels, seeking the curve of her breast. Her hands inside his unbuttoned shirt, spread against the hard, heated wall of his chest, registering the thunder of his heart.

He'd said her name hoarsely, and then, like a small uncertain echo, she'd heard 'Rhianna' spoken by a different voice, coming from an entirely different direction.

Her life had stopped. She'd turned sharply in disbelief and seen the small, slender figure standing, fragile and woebegone, in the doorway of the sitting room. Seen the dishevelled hair, the trembling mouth and the eyes swollen with tears.

'Donna?' She swallowed. 'What are you doing here?'

'I had to come back. I had nowhere else to go.' The other woman gave a little sob. 'Oh, Rhianna, I'm so sorry. Please try to understand…'

She looked past her at Diaz, a hand straying to her mouth. 'I— I thought you'd be alone. I didn't realise…'

'Don't worry about it.' Someone was speaking in her voice, Rhianna thought. Someone who sounded controlled and capable. Who wasn't dying inside, of disappointment and so many other things besides.

She said levelly, 'Donna, may I introduce Diaz Penvarnon? A cousin of my friend Caroline Seymour, whom I've mentioned to you.' And paused. 'Diaz, this is Donna Winston, a fellow cast member from *Castle Pride*. She was my flatmate until a short while ago, when she found—somewhere else.'

'Which clearly hasn't worked out,' Diaz said quietly. He didn't have to add, Exactly like tonight. But the words were there, all the same, hanging in the air between them, in all their regret and frustration. He said, 'I'd better go. May I call you tomorrow? Are you in the book?'

She wasn't, so she gave him her number hurriedly, watching as he logged it into his mobile phone.

Donna said with a catch in her voice, 'I'll make some coffee,' and trailed off to the kitchen.

Diaz took Rhianna in his arms, smiling ruefully down at her. 'I see the drama continues off-screen sometimes.' He paused. 'Man trouble?'

'It seems so.' *I know so.* She shook her head. 'Oh, God, I'm so sorry…'

'So am I.' His lips were gentle on hers. 'But we'll have our time, Rhianna. That's a promise.'

And even then, when it had all started to fall apart, she'd believed him.

He'd rung the next day. 'How's the friend in need?'

'Still needy,' she'd admitted, worn out after a night of tears, recrimination and seriously bad news, but feeling her heart lift when she heard his voice.

'And clearly around for the foreseeable future?' He sounded amused and resigned. 'I shall just have to be patient.' He paused. 'All the same, may I see you this evening? A film, maybe?'

'Yes,' she said, smiling foolishly into space. 'That would be lovely.'

Donna, having slept late, mooned tearfully round the flat most of the day. In the late afternoon she said she was going to see her agent, and departed.

Rhianna, sighing with relief, could only pray that she'd also visit a company arranging flat rentals.

Because she cannot stay here, she told herself, sinking gratefully into a deep hot bath. Not again, and not now. Things have gone too far, and she knows that.

She was still in her robe when the door buzzer went, and she looked at her watch and laughed, because he was nearly forty minutes early.

She was still smiling when she opened the door.

'Hello, Rhianna,' said Simon, and walked past her without waiting for an invitation. 'Are you alone? Good. Because it's time for a serious chat, I think.'

'Not now,' she said quickly. 'It—it's really not convenient. I'm expecting someone.' *The last person in the world who should find you here...*

'Tough.' He went into the sitting room, straight to the corner cupboard, and found the Scotch, pouring himself a generous measure.

When he turned, there was brooding anger in his face.

'I suppose she's told you?'

'Yes,' she said. 'Also that you've dumped her, accused her of getting pregnant deliberately in order to trap you, and ordered her to have an abortion. Nice work, Simon.'

'Of course you're on *her* side,' he said. 'All sisters together against the male oppressor. I know how it works. But don't be taken in by the innocent big brown eyes. She didn't need much persuading—as you must have noticed when you walked in on us that night.'

She hadn't forgotten. One of her rare migraines had threatened, sending her home early from a supper party. She'd heard noises from the sitting room and pushed open the door, to see Donna and Simon, naked and entwined on the rug in front of the fireplace, engrossed in vigorous and uninhibited sex.

Donna had seen her first and screamed. Simon had flung himself off his partner's body with more haste than finesse.

Rhianna had retreated to her room, sitting on the edge of the bed, fighting incipient nausea as the implications of what she'd interrupted came home to her.

She took a breath. 'Believe me, I'm on no one's side,' she said bitterly. 'But do you realise she was actually threatening suicide last night?'

'That's just ridiculous talk,' he said flatly. 'Ignore it.' He added, 'You do realise, I hope, that this baby simply cannot be born? I'm not going to lose all I want out of life just for one bloody stupid mistake.'

'Don't you mean a whole series of them?' She faced him, chin up, angry herself as she wondered defeatedly what had happened to the Simon she'd once known and whom, briefly and long ago, she'd thought she wanted.

I used to envy Carrie so much I was ashamed to look at her, she thought. Now I'm just ashamed.

She added fiercely, 'This is hardly a unilateral decision by you. A termination is incredibly serious for a woman.'

'And my future is equally serious,' he retorted, taking a gulp of whisky. 'For God's sake, Rhianna. You know what this would do to Carrie if she found out. That can't be allowed to happen. Admit it, damn you.'

'Yes,' she said bitterly. 'I know. And I swear she won't find out from me.'

'Good. Then you'll do whatever's necessary? Donna trusts you, and you can persuade her to do the right thing—if not for my sake, then for Carrie's.' He finished the Scotch and put the glass down. 'You're a great girl, Rhianna,' he went on more slowly. 'And you look bloody amazing in that robe. I'd bet good money you're not wearing anything underneath it. Care to prove it—for old times' sake?'

'There are no "old times"'. She looked at him with steady contempt. 'There never were. Now get out of here at once.'

He whistled. 'Hard words, but you're still going to help me, aren't you? Because you don't really have a choice.' He paused at the front door she'd thrown open. 'I'm relying on you, remember,' he added. 'So don't let me down.'

He turned to go, and she saw his face change. Looking past him, she realised that Diaz had indeed arrived ahead of time, and was standing motionless at the top of the stairs, his brows drawn together as he watched them.

'So this is the expected admirer,' Simon said mockingly. 'Well, well, you are a dark horse, Rhianna. I'll give your love to Carrie—shall I? Hello and goodbye, Diaz. Have a pleasant evening. I guarantee you will.' He winked at Rhianna and went, the sound of his footsteps clattering down the stairs.

Rhianna stood dry-mouthed as Diaz, still frowning, walked towards her, knowing that he would ask questions she would not be able to answer.

And felt the last remnants of hope shrivel and die inside her, as she had always somehow known they must.

As the flat door closed behind them, Diaz said abruptly, 'Does he make a habit of calling here?'

I don't want to lie to him. Please don't make me lie to him...
She said, 'He's around from time to time.'

'Carrie didn't say you were seeing each other.'

'She probably didn't think it worth mentioning.' Rhianna forced herself to play along and shrug lightly. 'After all, we're hardly strangers, he and I.'

'No,' he said slowly. 'I hadn't forgotten.' He paused. 'Is that how you usually receive him—dressed—or undressed—like that?'

'Of course not.' Her indignation at least could be genuine. 'And I certainly wasn't expecting him this evening, if that's what you think.'

'Frankly,' he said, 'I don't know what to think. After all, it was hardly the welcome I was anticipating.'

She looked away. 'Nor the one I'd planned, believe me.' Her voice was bleak.

He glanced around. 'So, where's the weeping willow?'

Rhianna bit her lip. 'That's neither kind nor fair.'

'Perhaps I'm not feeling particularly charitable. And you didn't answer my question.'

'She's gone out,' Rhianna said.

His brows rose. 'Good news at last,' he said softly. 'So, why don't we forget about the cinema and stay here?'

If she took two steps forward, she thought, she'd be in his arms, all questions silenced. He wanted her. She wanted him. Simple.

Except it was nothing of the kind. Because she knew, none better, the dangers of sex without any kind of commitment. She'd heard them being paraded only a little while ago, in this very room.

She was aware of her own feelings, but not his. Diaz was still an enigma to her. He'd spoken of her running away five years before, but he'd made no attempt to follow. He'd let her leave Penvarnon alone and, as far as he knew, friendless. It had been Francis Seymour and Carrie who'd stood by her, not him.

And he was here with her now only because of this nameless, inexplicable thing between them that had burst into life that night in the stable yard, subjecting her to the torments of the damned ever since.

Something apparently that he'd not been able to forget either, even as he lived his life, made his money and slept with other women.

An appetite in him that she'd aroused and he wished to satisfy. And when he'd taken all she had to give and he was no longer hungry—what then? What was to prevent him just walking away, leaving her used up and discarded? Like Donna?

And all on the strength of one short-lived and disastrous encounter when she was eighteen years old.

I'm worth, she thought, far more than that.

Aloud she said, 'Because Donna will be back very soon. So it appears that it's the cinema or nothing.' She added coolly, 'And in your present mood, Diaz, I have to say the second option seems preferable.'

'I could make you change your mind.'

Yes, but not my heart...

'Why, Mr Penvarnon,' she said mockingly, just as if she wasn't weeping inside, 'how very uncool.'

The look he sent her was long and totally deliberate, stripping away the concealing robe in order to create her nakedness in his imagination. And knowing what he was doing, and why, made it no easier to bear.

She stood, her body burning, hardly able to breathe, until at last he turned away, and she heard the outside door close behind him.

Then she sat down and covered her face with her hands.

She'd thought at the time that it was the nadir—the depths— the worst that could happen.

But I was wrong about that too, she told herself now.

She got up from the sofa, pushing her hair back from her face. She'd come down here to pack, she thought, not indulge in useless introspection. Therefore pack she would.

Be positive, she adjured herself. After all, there could hardly be more than another twenty-four hours for her to endure in his company. And if there was still a measure of physical attraction between them, then it could not be allowed to count. She didn't need it, and nor did he. *Finis*.

She opened the wardrobe and gave the selection of clothes there a jaundiced look.

She'd keep out her coffee linen dress, she decided, pulling a face, and stow the rest in her travel bag. But as she dragged it from the back of the cupboard it toppled over, and a medium-sized brown envelope slid out of the front pocket.

Rhianna picked it up, frowning. It was addressed to her, in handwriting she didn't recognise, she thought as she weighed it speculatively in her hand. Who on earth? And what on earth?

She wasn't in the mood for mysteries, but she couldn't help being curious all the same as she ran a finger under the flap. Inside she found a folder of photographs and a note.

She sat down on the bed, switched on the lamp, and read the note first.

Dear Miss Carlow,
We found this when we had the bedroom unit in the flat taken out. It must have fallen down behind it. We could see it belonged to your late aunt, and thought you might want to have it, so I put it with your things. I hope I did right.
M. Henderson.

So, Rhianna thought with a grimace, I seem to have a legacy from Aunt Kezia after all. How very weird.

She opened the folder and tipped out the handful of snapshots it contained.

It was an odd collection, all apparently taken round Penvarnon House and its grounds. None of the local views she might have expected. Just people. And clearly not posing. No one was smiling or saying 'cheese' because they'd glanced up and seen a camera on them.

And Aunt Kezia had been no photographer either. The angles were odd, capturing her subjects' back views, and the shots were hurried and blurred because the subjects were moving.

She studied them more closely, recognising Francis Seymour in several of them. But mainly they featured another man entirely, and for a bewildered moment she thought, It's Diaz. Why did she take all these pictures of Diaz?

Then she looked again, and realised that this was Diaz as he would be in ten or twenty years time—broader, heavier and greyer. But the resemblance was almost eerily strong, and she said, under her breath, 'Of course—it's his father. It's Ben Penvarnon.'

The next one showed a woman seated on the terrace at the house, her head bent, her body slumped, and it was only when Rhianna looked more closely that she realised she was sitting in a wheelchair.

How cruel, she thought, of Aunt Kezia to take a photograph of Esther Penvarnon, her employer, like this, and how unnecessary.

The rest all seemed to be of Moira Seymour, taken invariably from a distance and only just recognisable. In one she was standing near the top of the path down to the cove, glancing back over her shoulder, as if she knew there was a camera trained on her. In others she was emerging from the shrubbery, pushing the bushes aside, her face white and formless, or standing under the shadow of a tree with her husband.

There was something strange, even furtive about the photographs, Rhianna thought with distaste as she shuffled them together to replace them in the wallet. Then paused, because there was something else there. A slip of folded paper.

A cheque, she realised, for twenty-three pounds, made out to K. Trewint, and bearing the signature Benjamin Penvarnon. It was over twenty-five years out of date, and had clearly never been presented.

Rhianna stared at it in utter astonishment. How could her aunt possibly have overlooked such a thing? She'd have backed her to pay it into her account the same day—even if it had only been for twenty-three pence. So how could she have forgotten?

She refolded it and put it back in the wallet with the snaps, aware that her breathing had quickened. She felt as she'd done once when she was very young, when she'd turned over a stone in the garden only to release a host of creeping things that had scuttled everywhere. She'd screamed, knowing that if one of them ran over her sandal she wouldn't be able to bear it, and that she'd be sick or worse.

Now, she just felt—grubby in some odd way, wishing very much the bedroom unit at the stable flat had stayed where it was, with its secret intact.

Her instinct told her to destroy the entire folder, but she could hardly throw it overboard. It didn't seem fair to the dolphins. So she'd have to take it back to London with her and get rid of it there, she decided, tossing it back in her bag.

And now what she needed most in the world was a shower, she thought with a sudden shiver.

In the bathroom, she stripped and walked into the cubicle, rubbing handfuls of her favourite gel into every inch of her skin as if she were taking part in some essential decontamination process. Then she stood, head thrown back and eyes closed, allowing the cool, refreshing torrent to pour over her until every last trace of foam had gone.

She turned off the shower at last, with a sigh of relief and pleasure. Twisting her hair into a thick mahogany rope in order to squeeze out the excess water, she stepped back into the bathroom.

She'd heard no sound above the rush of the shower. Had felt no prickle of awareness. Yet he was there, standing in the doorway, watching her. Waiting for her.

She halted, hands still raised, totally, sublimely exposed, as a slow, quivering heat suffused her body under his silver gaze. As she acknowledged that it was much too late for even a token attempt to cover herself.

Nor was there any point in asking what the hell he thought he was doing there, because she already knew. But she had to say something—if only to break this taut and terrible silence stretching between them.

Her voice a husky whisper, she pleaded, 'Diaz—no…'

'You are so beautiful.' The words seemed torn from him. He moved, lithe as a panther, walking over to the pile of towels to take one and envelop her in it before, without haste, blotting the moisture from her skin.

'How can you do this?' she protested again, her voice shaking. The slow movement of his hands on her body through the layer of towelling was already an unbearable, shameful incitement. He was shirtless again, and the clean, sun-warmed scent of his skin filled her nose and mouth, turning her dizzy. 'Feeling as you do— despising me?'

'Because this is unfinished business between us, Rhianna, and you know it.' He spoke calmly. 'And whatever you've been to Simon Rawlins, it hasn't stopped me wanting you, although God knows I've tried.'

A fist seemed to clench inside her, and she knew she needed to stop him urgently, tell him everything before it was too late.

'Please,' she said, rapidly. 'Please, Diaz—you must listen. You don't understand…'

'No,' he said. 'You're the one who doesn't understand.'

He lifted her into his arms, stifling any further protest with the hard pressure of his mouth, and carried her into the other room. The coverlet on the bed had been turned back in readiness, and he put her down on the snowy sheet, followed her down.

Kneeling over her, he unwrapped the towel from her body and tossed it on to the floor. Stripped off his shorts and sent them to follow the towel, before stretching himself, naked, beside her.

'I need to erase him,' he told her quietly, almost conversationally, looking down into her widening scared eyes. 'To wipe him from your mind and memory for ever. To prove to you that you can't live in the past, Rhianna, and set you free. To show you that there's a present, and there can be a future.'

'No,' she said hoarsely. 'You're so wrong. There never will be—not without the man I love.'

He smiled with faint bitterness. 'You may be right,' he said. 'But at least I can try.'

He put his hand on her stomach, smoothing the damp skin with almost exquisite care, and she felt the pleasure of it shiver through every nerve-ending in her body.

'And you don't have to worry,' he added softly. 'I swear I'll be gentle.'

'Oh, God.' Her voice sounded stifled, caught as she was between terror and desire, as she realised what he meant. Remembered what he believed. 'Diaz—no. There's something I must say. Please let me go.'

'Yes,' he said. 'I will. As I promised. But not yet. We'll talk later. Afterwards.'

He leaned down and kissed her again, his lips moving on hers this time in a slow and seductive quest, coaxing them apart, preparing her for the heated, silken invasion of his tongue, carrying her, as some reeling corner of her mind acknowledged, beyond denial. But not beyond shame.

When at last he raised his head she was breathless, wordless, her pulses playing all kinds of tricks as she stared up at him through the veil of her lashes.

'I should have made love to you weeks ago,' he told her huskily. 'That night at your flat when I found him there. But I was too angry then. You were right to send me away. Before that you wanted me, and I knew it. Later, when I realised you were still sleeping with him, I told myself that it was too late—that I could never come near you—never bear to touch you again—not after—him.'

His mouth twisted. 'Yet here I am. Needing you so badly that I'm prepared to forget decency and reason, along with everything else that should be keeping us apart. I no longer have a choice.'

His stroking hand moved slowly upwards, over her midriff and ribcage, to cup the soft swell of her breast, his thumb grazing her nipple and awakening it to hot, aching life.

'We could even treat it as a pact,' he whispered. 'I'll release you from Simon and you, my lovely Rhianna, you can release me—from you. And maybe we'll both have some peace at last. Show me what you like.'

He bent, taking her tumescent rosy peak in his mouth, caressing it with the sweet agony of his tongue, making her gasp, her body arching involuntarily towards him.

She had only instinct to guide her. No prior knowledge of what the responses of her flesh might be to his hands and lips, or what he, in turn, might expect from her.

All those love scenes, taunted the only rational part of her brain still functioning. All that simulated ecstasy. And now that you're faced with reality instead of play-acting you haven't got a bloody clue...

And yet this is what you've longed for in all those long, empty years since you were eighteen—for Diaz Penvarnon to take you in his arms again and make love to you. To bring you to fulfilment as a woman.

No guilt. No shadows from the past. Just two people on a bed, together, just for a while.

And even if it is happening for all the wrong reasons, it's probably all you'll ever have of him—your one chance of happiness—so give him the only gift you have to offer and be thankful.

As if he'd picked up some unspoken cue, she heard him say, on a soft breath of amusement, 'This is usually a duet, sweetheart, not a solo. Aren't you going to touch me too? Let yourself remember how you once enjoyed being in my arms?'

She reached up to his shoulders, stroking the taut skin, feeling the strength of bone and the play of muscle under her shyly exploring fingers.

With a murmur of satisfaction Diaz drew her closer into his

arms, kissing her mouth again, while his own hands slowly traced the length of her long, supple spine, moulding the rounded curves of her buttocks.

She moved against him deliberately, the breath catching in her throat as she felt the answering pressure of his aroused hardness against her belly. She reached down, her fingers shyly seeking a more intimate acquaintance with all that iron male strength, but Diaz forestalled her, his hand on her wrist.

'Easy, my love,' he whispered, dropping light kisses on her eyelids, his lips tugging softly at her long lashes. 'I've waited far too long for this to be in any hurry, but God knows I'm only human, and I'm not sure how much of that particular delight I can bear right now. So let's—take our time.'

He began to caress her body, his fingertips brushing the creamy satin of her skin, and Rhianna lay, sighing through parted lips, her entire being subsumed in this glory of sensual pleasure he was creating for her.

And where his hands lingered his mouth followed, tasting the hollows at the base of her throat, the inside curve of her arms, the indentation of her navel, the faint swell of her hips and the slender length of her thighs.

She was moving restlessly beneath his touch, her flesh burning, eager for more. When his mouth took hers again she clung to him, her passionate response lacking all inhibition.

His lips returned to her breasts, suckling on their hard, aroused peaks, making her moan aloud, while his hand slid down to the shadowed cleft between her thighs and paused there.

He lifted his head and looked down at her, at the fever-bright eyes, the storm of excited colour along the high cheekbones, and the swollen, reddened mouth.

He said harshly, 'Do you still want me to stop? To let you go?'

'No.' Her voice was a shadow of itself. 'Oh, God—please—no…'

He began to touch her *there*, in the hot, secret centre of her, and she offered herself unequivocally to the intimacy of this new exploration, the mastery of his subtle fingers irresistibly enticing.

She'd never believed it could be possible to feel with such intensity, she thought as her breathing splintered, her mind and body focussed almost painfully on the sensuous stroke of his hand as he sought her tiny sheltered nub of sensitive flesh and brought it to aching delicious life.

Don't stop. The words were a silent scream in her head. *Never stop...*

Her body awash with fluid, scalding excitement, she heard him say hoarsely, 'Darling *now.*'

As he moved over her, above her, Rhianna obeyed instantly, clasping the rigid silken shaft of his virility with shaking fingers and guiding him into her with a little sob of anticipation.

Then, between one heartbeat and the next, everything changed. Because the last thing she'd expected was that it would hurt. That his physical possession of her would cause actual pain. The kind that made her flinch and tense into resistance, crying out before she could stop yourself.

Because that notion of virginity as a barrier to be breached was surely a myth belonging to past generations?

Yet here she was, with beads of perspiration on her forehead, sinking her teeth into her lower lip.

Diaz was suddenly very still. He said urgently, his breathing harsh and ragged, 'What is it? What's wrong? Darling, tell me...'

Then as he looked down at her, looked into her shocked, scared eyes, she saw realisation dawn—and a kind of horror.

He whispered, 'Oh, my God,' and lifted himself out of her—away from her—in one swift movement of utter finality, flinging himself on his side, his back to her, his breathing hoarse and ragged.

She lay staring at the ceiling, trying to say something—his name, perhaps, out of a throat tight with tears.

But eventually it was Diaz who broke the silence. 'You've never done this before.' It was a statement, not a question. He turned back slowly to face her, pulling up the sheet to cover the lower part of his body and propping himself on an elbow. 'Simon Rawlins was never your lover, and you're not having his child. Because until a few moments ago you were *virgo intacta.*'

'I'm sorry,' was all she could manage. 'I'm so sorry.'

'Yet, knowing that,' Diaz went on, as if she hadn't spoken, 'you encouraged me to—violate you. Why?'

She said, 'Because I wanted you.' *Because I love you. I always have and always will.*

Those unsayable words he would not want to hear. Therefore they went unsaid.

She took a deep breath. 'I decided long ago that my first time was going to be with someone I'd always really fancied, who knew what he was doing. You fitted the template perfectly—and created the opportunity too. You can hardly deny that. So it was never a—a violation. I truly wanted it, and you must believe that.'

She added unevenly, 'I thought being a virgin was simply a state of mind. I never dreamed there'd be—consequences.'

'Apart, you mean,' he said with chilling irony, 'from the dangers of unprotected sex? You didn't take those into consideration? The fact that there might be a real baby to be disposed of this time?'

She winced. 'Don't!'

Do you really imagine I'm capable of that? Especially if it's your child involved? I'd rather die...

'What the hell did you think you were doing?' he demanded. 'Taking part in some episode from that damned series? Making life up as you went along? Why in God's name didn't you tell me the truth about Simon Rawlins? Why did you let me think you were having an affair with him?'

For the first time she turned away from him, sheltering her naked body with the protection of her arms.

She said tonelessly, 'Because it was what you wanted to think. My mother took your father away from your mother. I had to be the one to take Simon away from Carrie. History repeating itself. Another ideal template.'

'No,' he said. Then, more forcefully, 'No, Rhianna, that makes no sense. You stood there and let me accuse you of being Simon's secret mistress without one word in your own defence. How do you explain that?'

He paused. 'You say you've always wanted me, but you went to great lengths to ensure we wouldn't be together.'

'No,' she said. 'Our joint family history did that. Because if it had ever become known we were lovers, all the old stories about my mother would have been dragged out for another airing. Her memory doesn't deserve that, whatever you believe.' She paused. 'Nor does your own mother, who is still around to be hurt. How would she feel if she knew you were sleeping with Grace Trewint's daughter?'

She stared sightlessly ahead of her. 'Maybe, unconsciously, when you started accusing me of being Simon's mistress I saw it as a convenient get-out clause—a means of escape from an impossible situation. And, perhaps what happened just now is fate's way of telling us that wanting each other still doesn't make it right.'

She bit down on her already torn lip. 'Would you go now, please? I—I'd rather be alone.'

'Tough,' Diaz said succinctly. 'Because I'm going nowhere.' He drew her back into his arms, swearing softly when he saw the expression of mute apprehension on her face. 'No, darling, I'm not planning to try and have sex with you again. I just need to hold you.' His mouth twisted. 'You look as if you need that too.'

It was suddenly all too much—the misery and disappointment, the knowledge that inevitably there'd be more questions to come, more blame assigned. The certainty that any remaining flicker of hope was gone for ever. Yet now, almost from nowhere, this unexpected kindness.

Rhianna turned her face into his shoulder and could taste the salt of his sweat on her trembling lips as she wept softly and bitterly in the arms of the man who could never be her lover.

CHAPTER NINE

AS SHE cried, she was aware of his hand smoothing her damp, tumbled hair, and his voice murmuring to her in a language she dimly recognised as Spanish.

And in some strange way both seemed equally comforting.

At last he lifted her and put her back against the pillows.

He said, 'I'm going to get you some water.'

'I'm not thirsty.'

'No,' he said. 'But you've bled a little.'

Her face burned. 'Oh, God, I'm so sorry,' she muttered, totally humiliated.

'Why?' Diaz dropped a kiss on the top of her head. *The kind of caress you'd offer a child.* 'I'm the one who feels like the biggest bastard in the known world.'

He reached for his shorts and zipped himself into them with a kind of finality.

When he returned from the bathroom she'd retrieved the towel from the floor and shrouded herself in it. She held out her hand for the cloth he'd brought, blushing again. 'Please—I'll do it.'

His hesitation was momentary, then he shrugged. 'If that's what you wish.' He added levelly, 'I assume it's also another way of asking me to give you some privacy?'

She looked away, nodding jerkily, and thought she heard him sigh.

'Then I'll go,' he said, and paused. 'But it's not over yet, Rhianna. We still have matters to discuss, you and I. You said so yourself.'

'But that was—before. I—I don't see what else you need to know,' she protested.

'Something quite simple really,' he drawled. 'It's known as the truth.'

He walked to the door and halted, looking back at her, his mouth twisting in a faint smile. 'Until later,' he promised, and went, leaving her staring after him, her eyes stricken.

Once alone, she sponged the tell-tale spots of blood from the sheet, then took another quick shower. Half an hour later, her hair dry, her face made-up, buttoned into the coffee linen dress, she was curled into the corner of the sofa, considering her options.

Which were few, she admitted wryly, and singularly unappealing.

Diaz wanted the truth. But what good could it possibly do—especially now that the marriage had taken place exactly as planned?

And particularly since he knew beyond all doubt that she'd never been Simon's mistress, or pregnant with his child. Why couldn't that be enough for him? Why did he need more?

Because nothing had changed. There was still a bitter, devastated girl out there who needed her support, no matter how tired she herself might be of the entire situation. How angry and sick at heart.

'Donna,' she whispered under her breath. 'Donna Winston. Oh, God, I wish I'd never met her. Never known of her existence.'

At the time, of course, it had all made perfect sense. The young actress had just won the role of governess Martha Webb in *Castle Pride*, and had wanted to move out of the noisy, over-crowded flat she shared with three other girls. Rhianna had had a spare room, which she'd offered as a temporary solution, while Donna looked around for a place of her own.

And at first it had gone reasonably well. Donna was also an only child, and they'd been careful to respect each other's space, although Rhianna had worked out fairly soon that the other girl, a year younger than herself, would probably never be a close friend. She was altogether too dependent, complaining constantly of being homesick, and spending a lot of time on the telephone to her parents in Ipswich.

One evening, after a hard day's rehearsal, they'd dropped into a local pizza place, too tired to face cooking at the flat. They'd finished their meal and were about to order coffee when a man's voice had said, 'Good God, Rhianna, fancy seeing you here.' She'd looked up to see Simon smiling at her.

It was far from the encounter of choice. She'd seen him several times when she'd been to Oxford, visiting Carrie, and had learned reluctantly to accept that they were very much an item again.

'Isn't this terrific?' Carrie had said happily one weekend when the three of them had been picnicking by the river. 'Just like old times.'

And Rhianna had seen Simon's eyes rest on her with a faint sneer, as if he was remembering that night in the stable yard and daring her to do the same. After which she'd made a conscious effort to time her visits when he was elsewhere.

A policy she'd pursued with reasonable success ever since. And the main reason she'd backed away from being a bridesmaid at the wedding, when Carrie had asked her months before.

'Simon—hi.' She tried to sound pleasant, but not unduly welcoming. 'Didn't Carrie tell me you were in Glasgow?'

'A temporary secondment,' he said. 'I came back a week ago.' He looked at Donna, assessing the heart-shaped face and enormous brown eyes, and his smile widened. 'Won't you introduce me?

She did the honours briefly, then signalled to the waitress to bring the bill.

'It seems we're having coffee at home,' Donna said with faint disappointment, then brightened, her eyes shining. 'I know— why don't you join us, as you and Rhianna are such old friends? Then you can catch up with each other's news.'

'I'd love to.' He turned to Rhianna, brows lifting. 'No objections, have you, sweet pea?'

Enough to fill a telephone directory, thought Rhianna.

'Of course not,' she said briskly. 'Although it will have to be a flying visit, I'm afraid. Donna and I have an early start tomorrow.'

'Well,' Simon said softly, 'instant coffee will be fine.'

She'd supposed afterwards that they must have swapped contact numbers while she was in the kitchen, because it had been within the following week that Donna's unaccountable absences had first begun.

But even then the penny hadn't dropped, Rhianna thought, because she'd seen Donna lunching in the canteen more than once with one of the assistant producers on the show, who was known to be something of a Lothario, and drawn her own conclusions.

I'm not her Mother Superior, she'd told herself, shrugging. If she wants to stay out all night with Hugh the Rover, she's entitled. She just doesn't seem the type, that's all.

She might have remained in the dark indefinitely, their unwitting and witless accomplice, but for that opportune headache.

She'd waited in her room that night until she heard the door slam behind Simon, then she'd gone in search of Donna. She'd found her crouching in a corner of the sofa, her dressing gown thrown round her, clutching a damp ball of a handkerchief in one hand. She'd looked at Rhianna with drowned eyes.

'I'm so—so sorry,' she gulped.

'Sorry?' Rhianna repeated incredulously. 'For God's sake, Donna, Simon's engaged to my best friend. The wedding's only a couple of months away. You know that perfectly well. The invitation's right there on the mantelpiece.'

Donna swallowed convulsively. 'Yes, I know. And Simon's told me all about it—how they were childhood sweethearts. But he's not going to go through with the wedding,' she added defiantly. 'He can't. Because he's fallen in love with me.'

'No,' Rhianna said bluntly. 'You're fooling yourself. Simon may be enjoying a bit on the side, that's probably the way he is, but he won't let Carrie go—not when push comes to shove. I can guarantee that. So stop this now, before you, and other people get hurt.'

'You're just jealous.' Donna rounded on her tearfully. 'You wanted Simon yourself years ago, and you made a really heavy pass at him. But you were found out, and as a result you got turned out of your own home by your aunt. He's told me all about it.'

'Then he's lied,' Rhianna told her icily. 'Not that it matters. You disgust me, the pair of you.' She took a deep breath. 'You'll have to move out, Donna. I can't let you stay after this.'

'So what are you going to do?' Donna demanded sullenly. 'Spill the beans to your little friend, I suppose?'

'On the contrary,' Rhianna returned curtly. 'I'm simply going to wait for Simon to come to his senses.'

Donna flounced past her to the door. She was gone within the hour—presumably to Simon. Rhianna didn't ask, and could only look forward to when the final episode of the current series was finished, and they didn't have to encounter each other on set any more.

Even so, she had to listen to the girl bragging about her gorgeous, sexy boyfriend, and how he was paying for her to meet up with him in Nassau.

Was Donna aware that she was simply an add-on to Simon's stag party in the Bahamas? Rhianna wondered wearily. And if so, did she care?

And then, several weeks later, Donna made that sudden unwanted reappearance back at the flat, confessing in floods of hysterical tears that she was pregnant, and that Simon had done a total and brutal about-face, telling her the affair was over and that she had to get rid of the baby.

'You were right about him,' she sobbed to Rhianna when they were alone. 'You said he'd marry her in the end. But I still love him. I can't bear to think of life without him. And how can he tell me not to have our child?'

Quite easily, Rhianna thought, when he'd never seriously considered relinquishing his commitment to Carrie. For him the baby was just a temporary inconvenience, to be dealt with swiftly and expediently.

The last thing she'd expected was to find herself dragged unwillingly into Simon's battle with Donna over the proposed termination, or to face its damning effect on her relationship with Diaz.

After the evening when he'd found her with Simon and walked out, she'd heard nothing from him for nearly two aching, unhappy weeks.

Then she'd gone to an opening night party for a friend from drama school in her first West End role, and Diaz, to her amazement, had been the first person she saw as she entered the room.

'What are you doing here?' she asked, her heart jolting pain-fully as he reached her side.

'I got a journalist friend to speak to your PR company,' he admitted ruefully. 'They said you'd be here, so I wangled an invitation.'

She looked at him uncertainly. 'Wouldn't it have been easier just to telephone me?'

'I tried that,' he said grimly. 'And I spoke to your flatmate who was doing her ongoing impression of a watering can. Something told me you might not get my message, so I decided to find a different way to make contact with you.'

Rhianna hesitated. 'Donna's not living with me,' she said. 'She comes round to see me because she's not—very happy.'

Not happy? She's totally hysterical most of the time, still threatening to harm herself. Sometimes I dare not let her be by herself...

'You amaze me,' he said. 'God preserve me from ever being in the vicinity when she's totally miserable.'

I wish I could tell you about it, she thought passionately. I wish I could go into your arms and unload the whole, horrible sordid mess and ask you to deal with it, because it's getting beyond me.

Yet I can't—I dare not. For Carrie's sake. Because even if you didn't half-kill Simon, you'd certainly do everything possible to stop the wedding, which would break her heart.

And it's still just possible that something can be saved from the wreckage, if I can just persuade Donna that Simon really isn't coming back. That even if the baby doesn't wreck her career, being a single mother in a chancy profession like acting isn't a sensible option. And besides, as she's said herself through floods of tears, it would destroy her mother.

Simon doesn't deserve Carrie, but maybe marriage will change him. Who am I to say that it won't? Maybe this thing with Donna has given him the scare he so badly needs, and he really will behave himself from now on?

I have to try and believe that, anyway.

She looked away from Diaz's intent gaze, afraid he would read the uncertainty and trouble in her eyes. 'Did you have something in particular that you wanted to say to me?'

'Yes,' he said. 'I need to apologise for my total overreaction the other night. I have no excuse except that Simon Rawlins has never been my favourite person.' His mouth twisted. 'Frankly, I find it hard to trust him.'

Her heart skipped a beat. *Oh, God, if you knew. If you only knew…*

She said in a low voice, 'Perhaps trusting isn't that big a deal where you're concerned?'

'I'd deny that,' he returned, unfazed. 'And so, I think, would the majority of my loyal and devoted staff around the world.' He paused. 'On the other hand they'd also tell you I don't cope well with being thwarted, although I appreciate that's no excuse for behaving like a bear with a sore head.'

She studied his waistcoat buttons with minute attention. 'Is that what you were? Thwarted?'

'Yes,' he said, his eyes lingering on her mouth. 'As you know perfectly well, my sweet, so don't play games.'

She shook her head. 'I—I don't think I know very much about you at all.'

'Well,' he said slowly, 'with your co-operation, I'm hoping to change all that.'

She looked back at him then, her eyes wide and candid. 'Do you think that's wise—given past history?'

'I wasn't considering wisdom,' he said. 'I had sheer necessity in mind. I thought you felt that too.' He allowed her an instant to digest that, then added more roughly, 'I'm not pretending it's going to be easy, Rhianna, but we'd be crazy not to try.'

'Or die in the attempt?' She tried to smile.

'I'd much prefer to live,' he said quietly. 'And with you.' He paused, glancing round. 'But there are a lot of people who also want to talk to you looking daggers at me, so don't answer me now. But soon—please.'

He reached for her hand and kissed it, his lips grazing the softness of her palm, making her whole body shiver.

She wanted to say, 'Take me with you. Take me—now.' But he was already turning away, and she could see an influential director bearing purposefully down on her, so realised she must wait for the glimpse of paradise that Diaz had offered her. The dream of joy, secretly nurtured for so long, and now astonishingly, incredibly, within her reach once more.

And she greeted the director with a smile so radiant that he almost jumped back in surprise.

She'd assumed that Diaz would stick around until they could leave together, and her heart sank when she suddenly realised that he'd already gone. Slipped away into the night at some point while she was talking to Helen, the euphoric lead in an undoubted hit.

As soon as she could she made her own excuses and left too. Sitting in the back of a cab, she let herself think about Diaz—how he'd looked, what he'd said, and the way his lightest touch could make her feel—until she tingled all over, wondering how soon she would see him again. Praying she would not have to wait too long. Teasing herself that she ought to be ashamed of her eagerness. Hoping that he would not be too disappointed when he realised she didn't have the experience he expected.

All the lights in the flat seemed to be on when she let herself in, and she halted abruptly, brows lifting, when she saw the dining table laid for two with her nicest lace placemats and crystal, and tall ivory candles already lit in their ceramic holders.

As Donna came in, carrying the salt and pepper shakers, Rhianna turned on her. 'Just what is going on here?'

'Simon's coming over.' The other girl's face had a sharp, intense look. 'He rang earlier, sounding completely different, and said he wanted to talk.'

'And you're cooking him dinner—here—in my flat?' Rhianna fought the sheer rage welling up inside her. 'Knowing how I feel about all that's happened—about him?' She punched a clenched fist at the ceiling. 'How dare you?'

She took a deep breath. 'Well, that's the end, Donna. From now on you're on your own. You can give me back the key you've been using and go.'

'Rhianna, please—let me stay—just one last time. Simon and I can't talk properly, not in that shoe box I live in, and I simply have to see him—don't you understand?' Donna's voice trembled. 'Something's changed with him. I know it has. And I have a really good feeling about it.'

'Which makes one of us.' Rhianna walked to the mantelpiece and took the embossed invitation wedged behind the clock. 'Recognise this?' She flung it on the table. 'The wedding is still going ahead, whatever you may think.'

She saw the other woman flinch, and, remembering her charged emotional state, made herself speak more gently. 'He's messing you around, Donna. Playing with your head. He won't give up Carrie and he wants you to go ahead with the termination, as agreed. In your heart you must know that.'

'Heart!' Donna spat the word. 'What would you know about hearts?'

'More than you think, perhaps.' Rhianna stalked to the bedroom, pulled out an overnight bag and began to fill it, swiftly and economically.

'What are you doing?'

'Getting out of here and going to a hotel. I can't throw you out physically, though I'd like to, but I'm damned if I'm going to hang around as if it's all right when it's all wrong.' Rhianna zipped her bag and swung it off the bed, giving Donna the look with which Lady Ariadne regularly curdled men's blood—and never to better effect.

'As it is,' she went on, 'you'll kindly get both of yourselves out of here when you've eaten. I'll be back by seven a.m. tomorrow, and I'd better not find you here.'

The hotel she went to had only a suite available, but as Rhianna slapped down her credit card she told herself it was worth every penny.

In the end she waited until gone nine o'clock the following morning before staging her return, to find the flat deserted and her bed ominously stripped.

She would consider the implications of that later, she told herself, drawing a deep breath.

The dinner table, however, had not been cleared, and although Rhianna wrinkled her nose at the used plates and cutlery, the crumbs and dribbles of wine, and the candle wax that had been allowed to spill down the holders, at least it was a mess she could deal with. Besides, it seemed a small price to pay in order to be rid of that precious pair and their squalid affair.

But don't rejoice too soon, she thought with sudden grimness. If Simon has changed his mind and they really are together permanently, how am I going to cope with the fallout? And how can I possibly explain my part in it all to Carrie? Come to that, what the hell will she do?

She went into the bathroom and began to run water into the tub.

'Survive,' she said aloud. 'That's what women do when they're dumped by the only men who'll ever matter to them. When they're torn and bleeding and stumbling around. They survive. Somehow.'

But please—please don't let it come to that...

She was clean, dry, scented and in her robe, making coffee in the kitchen, when the buzzer sounded.

Donna? she wondered ironically as she went to answer the door. Come back to lend a hand with the washing up, or offering to take the sheets to the launderette?

But it was Diaz who was waiting outside.

Diaz as she had never seen him before—heavy-eyed, unshaven, and still in the clothes he'd been wearing the previous night, minus the silk tie, and with his waistcoat and shirt unbuttoned.

'My God, what's happened?' She took a pace towards him and he stepped back, flinging up both hands as if to ward her off.

'Don't touch me,' he grated. 'Or I might do something we'll both regret for the rest of our lives.'

'I don't understand.' She stared at him. 'What's wrong?'

'You are,' he said. 'My sweet, treacherous Rhianna. Stringing me along. Encouraging me to make a total fool of myself. You're what's wrong. You—and Rawlins, of course.'

'You—you must be mad.' Her mouth was dry, her heartbeat quickening into panic. *He knows—but what does he know?*

'I was,' he said. 'But fortunately my sight wasn't affected. I saw him arrive last night, and let himself in with his own key. A very convenient and intimate arrangement.'

A key? Donna actually gave him his own key?

His eyes were on her face. He said harshly, 'It's all right, Rhianna, don't look so shocked. I know he's not here now, because I also saw him leave just after dawn. I was sitting in my car across the street, so I was able to time his visit to the minute.'

He threw back his head. 'And now I'm back again, to take a long look at you in daylight. No lamps, no candles, no moon, and no shadows for you to hide in.'

She could feel the anger radiating from him, hot and dangerous. She tried to say his name, but no sound would come.

He walked past her into the flat, into the living room, his mouth curling in distaste as he surveyed the debris on the table.

'A cosy dinner,' he observed flatly. He walked across to her bedroom, glancing at the unmade bed. 'Followed no doubt by an ecstatic end to a perfect day? I do hope, Rhianna, that you weren't also planning to share that bed with me?'

She found words. 'It's not what you think...' Oh, God, couldn't she have come up with something better than that hackneyed formula, usually employed when someone had been caught bang to rights? As he assumed she had.

'Did you tell him I wanted you too, Rhianna? Did you share that with him during pillow talk, or were you too preoccupied?' He shook his head. 'You should have dumped him for me, darling. I'm a very rich man and I'd have paid a great deal for the pleasure of you. Actresses, even with bodies as lovely as yours, are two a penny. You could have made a small fortune allowing me access to that treacherous, delectable little body of yours. Used it as your pension fund when your other work eventually dried up.'

He added mercilessly, 'You've used me. Just as your mother used my father, years ago.' He gave a short mirthless laugh. '"Past history", you said. The pair of you, mother and daughter, unable to keep your greedy, selfish hands off other women's men, and I wouldn't let myself see it.'

He drew a breath. 'All this time—cheating on Carrie. Pretending to be her friend when you were out to steal her fiancé. I should have remembered that you're an actress, trained to deceive. You're even better in real life than you are on television.'

Last night's receipted hotel bill, she thought, showing the hot chocolate she'd ordered last thing from Room Service and this morning's breakfast, was in her bag. She only had to show it to him to throw his accusations back in his face.

Except that it wouldn't stop there, she realised just in time. Because if *she* hadn't been with Simon last night, then someone else clearly had. And he would want to know who that was.

She swallowed. 'Are you going to—tell Carrie?'

It was all she could ask. She'd been drawn into this disaster by the need to shield her friend from the knowledge that Simon had enjoyed a blatant and cynical affair only weeks before their wedding. She still needed to do that. Now she had to discover the terms.

'No,' he said. 'How can I? I hold no brief for Rawlins, but it's the fact that he cheated on Carrie with you that sticks in my gullet. Although I can't blame him, or any other man, for being tempted. I haven't exactly been immune myself,' he added curtly. 'I've seen the way you move, the shape of your mouth. Those eyes a man could drown in. Who wouldn't want to get you into bed?'

He shook his head. 'But you were supposed to love her, Rhianna. You should have said no. I can't bear her to know how you've betrayed her.'

She said quietly, 'No, I can see that. Thank you.'

She saw him look past her and realised that the wedding invitation was still lying on the table, where she'd tossed it earlier. Diaz picked it up and tore it into small fragments, which he dropped on to a dirty plate.

'You will not come to the wedding,' he said, his eyes cold steel. 'Do you understand me? You'll make some excuse. I don't care what it is. But you'll bloody stay away—from my home and my family. And especially from Carrie, before and after her marriage. That friendship ends now. Because I don't trust you, Rhianna. This might have been a casual fling for Rawlins, but you're still sleeping with him, which makes me suspicious that you might have your own agenda where he's concerned. Not on my watch. You keep your distance, and your mouth shut, Rhianna, or you'll be sorry. Don't say you weren't warned.'

He walked to the door. 'I've decided to return to South America tomorrow,' he said. 'So with luck we won't meet again.' His smile made her shiver. 'Just pray that we don't.'

And he went out, leaving her standing in the ruin of her life, her arms wrapped defensively round her shaking body.

And now they had met again, and it seemed that she was going to have all the opportunities for regret that could possibly be crammed into one lifetime.

Circumstantial evidence had amazing power, she thought bleakly. Seemingly incontrovertible facts, piling up against her like great stones. Crushing her and silencing her.

Her only—her ultimate—defence had turned out to be the physical innocence she'd surrendered to him on that bed. Ironically, when it no longer mattered.

But the fact that she'd been a virgin did not mean there'd suddenly be bluebirds flying over the rainbow.

Because all the old problems between them hadn't gone away. In fact they'd probably been compounded by her abject failure to keep him at arm's length.

And they still had no future.

Sighing, she got to her feet. She couldn't stay down here for ever, as if she was too shy or too scared to face him. Once she'd seen to her delayed packing she would go up on deck and do her best to seem calm and collected, as if the events of the past two hours had never occurred. Or were somehow no big deal.

Smoke and mirrors, she thought. Playing a part she would never have chosen in a million years. So that soon, maybe within a day or two, she could walk away from him for ever, without looking back or letting him see how high a price she was paying for her departure.

Diaz was sitting at the table under the awning, looking out to sea, but at her approach he rose politely. He'd changed too, she saw, into close-fitting chinos and a dark blue shirt, open at the neck, sleeves turned back.

Realised too that just the sight of him was enough to send her spinning into some infinity of pain mingled with a desire that was no longer just a figment of her imagination but a recently experienced reality.

God help her, she could still taste his mouth on hers, feel the warm arousal of his hands on her breasts and thighs. Could recall in every detail the sheer impetus of need that had driven her to surrender such a short time ago.

It took all the courage she possessed to walk forward and join him now, wryly aware as she was that her swollen nipples were chafing against the confines of her bra, and that a soft languorous ache was coming to slow life deep within her all over again.

As she sat, he indicated a jug filled with deep red liquid, clinking with ice cubes and afloat with lemon slices, that stood in front of him.

'Enrique concocts a lethal sangria,' he remarked. 'Are you prepared to risk it?'

She shrugged. 'Why not?'

It would make as good an anaesthetic as any other, and she needed all the help she could get, not just for the next few hours, but for the remainder of whatever time she had to spend in his company.

I wish I could fall asleep, she thought, and wake up in London with all of this behind me, so that I could begin to put myself together again. Rebuild my life and plan for some kind of future. Find another dream—if that's possible...

In the meantime... 'Any more dolphin sightings?' she asked brightly, trying not to gasp as the sangria hit home.

'Sadly, no, but they may be waiting to catch another glimpse of you.' He paused. 'I like your dress.'

'You've seen it before.'

'Ah,' he said lightly, 'but perhaps I wasn't in the mood to appreciate it at the time.'

There seemed no answer to that, so she took another cautious sip of sangria.

'Be careful,' he warned lazily. 'I don't want you to pass out on me.'

And there was definitely no answer to that, Rhianna decided, staring resolutely down at the table. She needed a neutral topic of conversation, and quickly.

'What happens in the morning?' she said. 'When we get to Puerto Caravejo?'

'We may have to wait for a flight,' he said, after a pause. 'So I thought I'd show you my house.'

'Goodness,' she said. 'You have a castle in Spain as well?'

'Is that what you're expecting?' His tone was dry. 'Then you'll be disappointed. It's little more than a farmhouse which, unlike the rest of our family estate in the Asturias, managed to survive the Civil War. It's been extended since then, but it's still more comfortable than luxurious.'

She digested that. 'Do you spend a lot of time there?'

'Not as much as I could wish,' he said. 'But all that will change when I finish disposing of our assets in South America.'

She put down her glass. 'But I thought that was where your real home was? Where you spent most of the year?'

'It has been,' he said. 'But I decided some time ago that my life needed to be simplified. Racing from one side of the globe to the other isn't much fun any more. And nor is being saddled with an armed guard much of the time,' he added with a touch of grimness. 'Besides, the mineral workings are coming to the end of their natural span anyway, and the land can be used for other purposes.'

'But you'll miss the travelling, surely?'

He shrugged. 'The consultancy is growing each year, and although I have a great team I'm still actively involved, so that should take care of any lingering wanderlust. For the rest of the time I plan to put something back into my land in Spain. Plant more apple orchards, maybe some vines. A friend of mine made the Rioja we drank the other night, and he offered a while back to teach me the wine business. So in many ways I'm going to be busier than ever.' He paused. 'Then there's the reclamation project at Penvarnon.'

'You're going to rebuild it?' she asked uncertainly.

'Not with bricks and mortar,' he said. 'I intend to—take it back. Spend much more time there. Make it mine. I've only allowed the present situation to drag on like this because it's suited my convenience. My uncle's always understood that, and he'll be relieved to go. He's never been happy there.'

She said without thinking, 'It's never been a happy house.'

'No,' Diaz said, after a pause. 'Which is something else I mean to change.' He leaned back in his chair. 'And, while we're enjoying this full and frank exchange of information, my sweet, you can start telling me about your tearful little friend Donna Winston. In particular how long she and Simon Rawlins have been sleeping together and why you kept quiet about it. Because that's something I really need to know.'

CHAPTER TEN

For a long moment Rhianna was silent, then she said quietly, 'How did you know it was Donna?'

'I realised a little while ago,' he said. 'When I was in the shower. Great places, showers, for clearing your head and getting you to think straight.' His mouth twisted. 'So, I used the time-honoured method of adding two and two, and arrived, for once, at the correct answer.'

He shook his head. 'God in heaven, how could I have been so dumb? "Man trouble". I said it myself, the night I met her.' He looked at her unsmilingly. 'And you said, "It seems so." Only you *knew*, Rhianna. You knew exactly what was going on, yet you said nothing. You even condoned the affair by letting them meet at your flat.'

'Never.' She looked back at him, her eyes fierce. 'And I didn't know—not at first. We bumped into Simon in a pizza place one night, quite by accident, and he deliberately inveigled an invitation back for coffee—the last thing I wanted, as he very well knew. Relations between us had been cool for a long time, and I'd have crossed busy streets to avoid him. I was probably too damned annoyed at being manipulated like that to pick up any other nuances.'

She paused. 'Then I just happened to walk in on them one night—and caught them *in flagrante*. After he left there was a confrontation between me and Donna. She claimed they were in love. I advised her to think again, and told her to go. But later I started feeling almost sorry for her—because I'd introduced them, after all, and she probably thought Simon was a friend of mine who could be trusted. Or maybe she'd turned him into some romantic golden-haired hero—the way you do when you're young and silly.' She bit her lip. 'I can hardly blame her for that. There was a time when I thought he was wonderful too.'

'That,' he said, 'had not escaped my attention.'

She said swiftly, 'If you're thinking of Carrie's birthday party, then you're so wrong. I was over him long, long before that.'

'Then why go to meet him?'

'Because he said—he made me think Carrie would be there too. I'd never have gone otherwise.' She bent her head. 'I know how it must have looked.'

He said, 'I didn't give you much chance to explain. But why didn't you tell me what was going on that evening when I arrived at the flat and found him with you?'

She sighed. 'Because I could have been opening Pandora's box. The consequences might have been awful. Besides, Simon kept insisting it was all over between them, that he'd learned his lesson and it was only Carrie that he wanted. And I—I wanted so badly to believe that. Because I couldn't convince myself that she'd be happier without him. Better off, maybe—probably—but not happier. So,' she added unhappily, 'I took the coward's way out and hoped it would all simply go away—that no one else need ever know.'

His brows rose. 'So you were trying to keep the peace? Is that it?'

'No,' she said. 'I can't even claim that.' She took a breath. 'The fact is—I was frightened. I can make all the excuses in the world, but that's what it comes down to in the end. I told myself that if I said nothing I'd be protecting Carrie, saving her from this terrible hurt, when all the time I didn't want to be the one to tell her.'

She looked down at the table. 'In the old days they used to kill messengers who brought bad news, and I was scared that I'd lose her too—lose our precious friendship. For so long it was all I had, and I was afraid that she'd never forgive me if I was the one to destroy her illusions about Simon and break her heart.'

He said, 'That's not such a bad reason. Except, of course, it didn't all go away.'

'No,' she said. 'Donna had come back that night to tell me she was pregnant, and Simon wanted her to have an abortion. She was going to pieces right there in front of me, so I could hardly throw her out. She had her own place, but she virtually moved back in with me, just weeping hysterically and refusing to eat or get dressed half the time. She kept her key too, and must have had it copied for Simon—though I didn't realise that until too late.'

She added flatly, 'I don't think they ever really stopped seeing each other. Not even when he was accusing her of deliberately getting pregnant because she knew he was going to finish with her, and she was threatening to take an overdose or cut her wrists if anyone mentioned termination. Eventually she calmed down enough to make an appointment at a clinic, but she told Simon she'd only go through with it if I went with her. He's been hassling me over that ever since. Or until yesterday, anyway.'

She frowned. 'I haven't actually seen Donna since the night Simon stayed at the flat, so I don't know her current stance. And in spite of everything I haven't been able to lose all sympathy with her.'

He said, 'Then you must have the patience of a saint.'

'No.' She looked out to sea. 'It—it's not—it can't be easy to accept that you're never going to have the one man who means everything to you. And I think she did fall for him very badly, and believed that he loved her too.'

'A little naïve,' he commented.

'Yes.' Rhianna was silent for a moment. She added reluctantly, 'Although Simon did claim originally that *she'd* targeted *him*, and made all the running.'

'Hardly a reliable authority,' he said unsmilingly.

'No, but plausible—and it made me wonder. Because Rob, who's usually kindness itself to newcomers on the cast, avoided her like the plague. And when he heard she was moving into the flat he told me that she was a damned sight older than her age, and infinitely more streetwise, and warned me to be careful.'

'What I still need to know,' Diaz said slowly, 'is why you let me think you were the one involved with that two-timing bastard?'

'Because it seemed the one way to guarantee you wouldn't tell Carrie either.' She met his gaze. 'I couldn't believe you'd cause her more suffering by letting her know she'd been betrayed not just by Simon but by her best friend too. I was certain that her peace of mind would be far more important to you than your contempt for me. It was more important to me too.'

'But you stood there,' he said, 'and you let me say those foul, unforgivable things to you.'

'Because I was involved in it.' She spread her hands almost helplessly. 'I couldn't deny that. And I hadn't been able to do a thing to stop it. I couldn't even pretend that it was just one of those things that happens when people have had too much to drink.'

He lifted a hand and smoothed a strand of hair back from her face. 'About which you know so much, of course,' he said, his voice caught between tenderness and amusement.

'I don't think I know very much at all,' she said, as her pulses leapt in unbidden, dangerous delight. 'About anyone or anything. I'm better with someone else's script.' She paused. 'Would you have kept quiet—to spare her feelings—if I'd told you the truth? I felt I couldn't take the risk—especially when you were so angry.'

'No,' he said quietly. 'Probably not.'

'Well, then,' she said. 'Maybe it's all turned out for the best.'

'I wish I shared your optimism,' he returned drily. 'Whatever, it's too late now. They'll be off on their honeymoon.'

He reached across, and took her hand, playing gently with her fingers. 'So—do you forgive me?'

'For saying what you did?' She was embarrassed to hear the sudden quiver in her voice that his touch had engendered. 'Of course. In some ways I deserved it.'

Diaz shook his head, smiling faintly. 'Not just that.'

'Oh,' she said, trying to ignore the dismaying fact that she was also blushing. 'You mean *that*.'

'Indeed I do,' he agreed.

Rhianna tried unsuccessfully to free her hand. 'Couldn't we simply forget it ever happened?'

'Not a chance,' he said. 'Because I don't want to forget.' He added drily, 'Nor do I wish you to have that as your abiding memory of me as a lover.'

She was trembling inside. 'Please don't say things like that.'

'That sounds ominous.' He sent her a searching look, then raised her hand to his lips, kissing her fingertips very gently. 'Has our recent encounter put you off for life? I do hope not.'

'No. I mean—I don't know.' She was stumbling now, and Lady Ariadne's glamorous self-possession had never seemed further away. 'But I—I must have been a terrible disappointment.'

'No, my sweet,' Diaz said, and smiled at her. 'Believe me, that couldn't be further from the truth. My sole regret is that I didn't know it was your first time, or I would have dealt with the matter rather differently.'

'Oh,' she said, wondering how, and knowing she could never ask.

She rallied. 'Anyway, it's all over now, and in a few hours we'll be in Spain and I'll be leaving. So maybe what happened is all for the best too.'

His smile widened into a reluctant grin. 'Not from my point of view, darling. Nor, I'd have said, from yours. However,' he went on, more gently, 'if you give me the chance, I think I can guarantee you more enjoyment next time.'

Hunger for him—for the intimate riches he was offering—clenched like a fist inside her.

But at the same time she knew it would be infinitely safer to starve. Because all he was proposing was a consummation—the satisfaction of a mutual desire.

And she wanted all of him. For ever. It was that simple. And that impossible.

Was this how Donna wanted Simon? she wondered, and realised why, in spite of everything, she'd found herself pitying the girl who'd given everything to a man she adored and watched him take it and walk away.

Because Diaz would be no different, she told herself. He had no choice in the matter. They were who they were. His father's son, her mother's daughter. Nothing could alter that.

But at least he'd been honourable enough not to pretend, or to make promises he wasn't prepared to keep.

He might want me, she thought, but he's never mentioned love.

He said he wanted to wipe Simon from my mind for ever and erase his own need for me at the same time. And maybe he can do that. But I—I can't. I might not have known it then, when I was in his arms, but I do now.

And when I told myself it was enough—that I would make it enough—I was lying. I can't let myself be chained to him for the rest of my life by the memory of a night's pleasure.

I need to save myself. Somehow.

She released her hand from his clasp and sat back. 'I don't think so,' she said, her answering smile polite, even faintly regretful. 'But thank you, anyway. Because you've helped me to achieve what I wanted. Some uncommitted experience, without any untidy emotions in the way.'

She paused. 'So please don't feel guilty that you didn't make the earth move. After all, it was hardly likely under the circumstances. And now my curiosity's been satisfied, at least, so I'll know what to expect in future—what the possibilities could be. I'd much prefer to settle for that—for the time being.'

She shrugged gracefully. 'Everything else can wait until I fall in love.'

There was a silence, then Diaz said expressionlessly, 'How neat. How tidy.'

She looked away. 'Maybe the events of the past few months make order and decency in my life seem strangely attractive.' She added abruptly, 'I'm sorry.'

'Don't be.' It was his turn to shrug. 'It's your decision, and I can't argue with that—much as I'd like to. Because I suspect that with you, Rhianna, those possibilities you mention could be endless.'

He paused. 'But I hope at least you'll allow me to kiss you goodbye when the time comes?'

'Why not?' She drank some more sangria, praying she'd never be obliged to touch it again as long as she lived, because it would always—always—bring this moment back.

The time I did the right thing, she thought, and felt myself die inside.

She added, 'I know we probably won't see each other again after this, but I'd like us to part friends. If we can.'

'A nice thought,' he said silkily. 'But hardly feasible. Under the circumstances.'

He emptied his glass, pushed his chair back and rose. 'Dinner will be early this evening, and I suggest you get some rest after it. You won't get much sleep once we reach port.'

He hesitated, looking down at her. 'And if you're speaking from someone else's script, you need more rehearsal. Because right now it doesn't work. Not for me, and probably not for you either.'

He added flatly, 'I'll see you later,' and walked away to the bridge.

Dinner was paella, produced by Enrique with a delighted flourish, and Rhianna smiled and said, 'How wonderful,' and ate her share, even asked for more—although every mouthful tasted like cardboard, and her stomach was twisted in knots anyway.

She'd expected it would be a quiet meal. That after her rejection of him Diaz would not have a great deal to say to her, but she was wrong. Clearly his male pride hadn't been dented too badly, she told herself wryly, as he chatted lightly, amusingly, and above all impersonally, keeping the topics of conversation general, and making it easy for her to pick up a similar tone.

While in between, very carefully, ensuring that his attention was safely on his food, she watched him from under her lashes with passionate concentration, etching every line of his dark, mobile face into her consciousness, then closing it away in some secret compartment in her mind which she could unlock sometimes. Not every day, she promised herself. Just when the loneliness and the need became too much to bear.

'Tell me something,' he said suddenly, when the coffee had been placed on the table and Enrique had returned to the galley. 'What made you choose acting as a career?'

'It was something I'd always loved to do,' Rhianna said, after a startled pause to register that they'd moved from impersonal to personal again. 'But my aunt had different views, so I didn't have much opportunity until I went back to London. There were evening drama classes at one of the education centres, and I went along.'

She shrugged. 'My teacher thought I had something, and arranged for me to audition at stage school. I got a place, plus a bursary I never knew existed. And the people I was living with—the Jessops—were absolutely wonderful, and refused to take a penny from me while I was training.'

She bent her head. 'I can't help imagining sometimes how different my life would have been if they'd been allowed to foster me when my mother died. They wanted to, but Aunt Kezia insisted on taking me away. I never understood why, because she never wanted me or even liked me. She made that quite clear. And she inflicted me on a place where she knew I'd be unwelcome, when there was no actual need.'

She sighed. 'I've never been able to figure it.'

He said quietly, 'She was certainly a strange woman.'

'Stranger than you know.' Rhianna paused. 'Apparently she used to take these really terrible, pointless photographs of people, as if she was deliberately catching them off-guard.'

His brows lifted. 'What people?'

'Your aunt and uncle,' she said, adding reluctantly, 'And your father. There are lots of your father.' *And your mother in a wheelchair, but I'm not mentioning that. Or the cheque. In fact I wish I'd said nothing about them at all.*

'You have these photographs?'

'The Hendersons found them at the flat and passed them on to me.' Her mouth twisted. 'My sole Trewint legacy.'

'Not quite,' he said. 'You have that amazing hair, like some beautiful dark red cloud. That's an inheritance to treasure.'

Which was altogether too personal, Rhianna decided. She finished her coffee and rose.

She said politely, 'If you'll excuse me? I think I'll take your advice and get some sleep.' And turned away, only to find him beside her at the companionway.

She said crisply, 'I know my own way, thanks.'

'Of course,' Diaz said, and smiled at her. 'But you seem to have forgotten you promised me a kiss.'

Her heart thudded. 'When we said goodbye,' she returned. 'That was my understanding of the agreement.'

'But there's always such hassle at airports,' he said softly as they reached her door. 'Let's make it goodnight instead.'

She hesitated uneasily. 'Well—if you insist.'

It's a kiss. That's all. Don't make a big deal about it, or let him see it matters. Just get it over with.

'Well, yes,' he said, faint amusement in his voice. 'I think I do.' He reached for the handle and opened her door.

She gave him a startled glance. 'But there's no necessity for that. Right here and now will be fine.'

'Except that I prefer privacy,' he said. He picked her up and carried her into the stateroom, kicking the door shut behind him. 'And comfort,' he added, putting her down on the bed and coming to lie beside her.

'You said *a kiss*,' she reminded him, her voice shaking.

'Did I specify a number?' He drew her to him. 'I don't think so.' He lifted a strand of scented hair and carried it to his mouth. He said gently, 'You are loveliness itself.'

He began to kiss her without haste, his mouth touching her forehead, her eyes, her cheekbones, the soft vulnerability below her ears, and the trembling corners of her mouth.

His lips were warm as they parted hers, and infinitely beguiling. His tongue began a lingering silken quest of the inner contours of her mouth, and her breath sighed with his. He gathered her closer, holding her against the hard length of his body, letting the kiss deepen slowly, endlessly.

When she could speak, she whispered brokenly, 'Diaz—this isn't fair.'

'I'll spare us both the obvious cliché.' He put his mouth against her throat as his fingers began to release the long row of buttons at the front of her dress. 'If this is all I'm to have of you, Rhianna, then I intend to make the most of it. And I'm still only kissing you,' he added huskily. 'Even if it's not how—or where—you expected.'

As the edges of her unfastened dress fell apart, Diaz looked down at her for a long moment, then bent, his lips brushing the creamy swell of her breasts as they rose from their lacy confinement.

Lifting her slightly, he freed her from her dress, tossing it to the end of the bed, then dealt with the hook of her bra, taking the tiny garment from her body and sending it to follow her dress.

He began to kiss her breasts, circling her nipples with the tip of his tongue, bringing them to hot, aching life, before taking each soft, scented mound into his mouth and laving their tumescent peaks with slow, voluptuous strokes that made her moan aloud.

His lips moved down her body, leaving a trail of fire over her ribcage and the flat plane of her stomach, his tongue teasing the whorls of her navel, while his hands deftly removed her remaining covering of silk and lace as if brushing aside a cobweb.

It was only then that Rhianna realised where this downward path was leading, and as his mouth reached the silky triangle at junction of her thighs she stiffened in panic, her fingers tangling in his hair as she tried to push his head away.

'No!' She choked the word. 'God—no…'

Effortlessly Diaz captured her wrists, holding them at either side of her shocked body, before he bent to her again, kissing the smooth length of her thighs, and their soft inner flesh, every brush of his lips a silent enticement, coaxing them to part for him, until she could resist no longer and sank, sighing, into the promise of this new and startling intimacy.

His mouth took possession of her with a gentleness that was almost reverent, kissing the secret woman's flesh she had yielded to him, then slowly and sensuously deepening the caress into explicit exploration.

His tongue was a quiet flame flickering against her, at one moment probing delicately into her innermost self, at the next seeking out her tiny hidden bud and urging it to swollen, delicious arousal.

Offering her with patience, tenderness and untiring, unhurried grace, a glimpse of an unknown, undreamed-of world of pleasure.

Time was suspended. There was only this endless—exquisite—torment. This intolerable, unceasing delight. She was consumed by sensation, conscious of it building inside her with all the irresistible force of a giant wave. Aware that each lingering, sensual stroke of his tongue was carrying her away, sweeping her inexorably, helplessly, towards some trembling, anguished pinnacle.

And when the wave broke, and she was flung out into some shimmering, shattering void, she heard herself cry out in sobbing triumph at the glory of her first sexual release.

Diaz wrapped her in his arms, his hand cradling her head, until she stopped shaking and her body began to relax into peace.

When she could speak, she said, 'Is—is it always like that?'

'I don't know,' he returned softly. 'I'm not a woman. But I hope so.'

She remained still, her lips against the column of his throat, her hand pressed to the wall of his chest, feeling the thud of his heartbeat through his shirt, thinking dreamily she'd be content to stay where she was for ever.

Yet at the same time it occurred to her that there was an incongruity about being naked in his arms when he was still fully dressed that made her feel almost shy. And how ridiculous was that, considering what had just taken place?

She reached up and began to unfasten his shirt, but he halted her.

'Not now, my sweet.'

'But don't you want…?'

'Yes,' he said. 'But later. When we have all the time we need.' He kissed her eyes and, gently, her lips. 'Get some sleep now, and I'll wake you when it's time to go ashore.'

He lifted himself off the bed and covered her with the sheet, stroking her damp hair back from her forehead.

He said again, 'Later,' the promise repeated in his smile, and went.

CHAPTER ELEVEN

THE first thing Rhianna noticed when she opened her eyes was that the light was different. The next that the room wasn't moving. The third that she was in a much bigger bed than the one on *Windhover*.

She was also alone, although the crumpled pillow beside her and the thrown-back covers demonstrated that this had not always been so.

She sat up, yawning, and considered her new environment.

Her actual arrival in Spain remained something of a blur. She could recall there'd been certain formalities to undergo before they'd been free to make their way to the car waiting on the quayside. The driver, an undeniably handsome lad, called Felipe with smouldering eyes and a sulky mouth, had stared at Rhianna with undisguised admiration until a quiet word from Diaz had recalled him to his duties.

It had been too dark to form any impression of the countryside they'd travelled through, and eventually, supported by the comfort of Diaz's shoulder, she'd dozed again.

She hadn't absorbed much about the house either, apart from being greeted by a stout woman with greying hair, who'd watched with an expression of faint disapproval when Diaz had swung her off her feet and carried her upstairs to this room.

She had a dim memory of him sliding into bed beside her at some point, and of turning into his arms with a murmur of pleasure. But after that—nothing.

And now here she was, all by herself.

For a moment a cold hand seemed to brush her skin, but she shook the feeling away. It was too late for regrets—for wishing that last night had not happened. No point in telling herself it had been a matter of male pride to show her that after pain there could be pleasure. Or that he'd tricked her.

She was out of her depth and drowning with all she felt for him, and she'd change nothing—apart from wishing he'd been with her when she woke.

She lay back against the pillows again, and looked around her with growing pleasure. It was a large room, its pale walls the colour of aquamarine, which appeared even more spacious because of the few items of furniture it contained. Apart from the bed there was only a large wardrobe and a tall chest of drawers, elaborately carved in some dark wood, and two smaller matching tables flanking the bed.

The shutters at the long windows were slightly open, and a bright shaft of sunlight was spilling across the tiled floor, while the drapes of unbleached linen stirred in the faint breeze.

Opposite the bed was a door leading to a bathroom, judging by the glimpse of azure tiles and creamy marble beyond.

What she couldn't see anywhere was her luggage. Even the things she'd been wearing last night had disappeared.

But perhaps they were in that enormous wardrobe.

She got out of bed and, for want of anything better, took the sheet with her, winding it round her body in case the woman with pursed lips, whose name she recalled was Pilar, should suddenly reappear.

But the wardrobe and drawers contained only male attire, proving that this lovely room belonged to Diaz.

She padded into the bathroom, which was equally pleasing. As well as the powerful shower in its glass-walled cubicle, there was a deep bathtub, and twin handbasins set side by side in a marble-topped unit.

Indicating, she thought, swallowing, that she wasn't the first to share his room. But she wouldn't think about that—nor about the other women before her who must have sobbed their rapture into his shoulder. Or those who would follow her into his bed.

Particularly not those, she thought, fighting a sudden twist of pain as she headed back to the bedroom. Because that way lay madness.

'Rehearsing for *Julius Caesar*?'

At the sound of his voice Rhianna turned, almost tripping on her trailing sheet. He was lounging in the doorway, his mouth curved in amusement, the towel draped round his hips his only apparent covering.

'Auditioning for *Tarzan*?' she retorted.

'No chance,' he said. 'All that swinging through trees is far too strenuous. I'd have saved my strength for Jane.' He paused. 'You were sleeping like a baby, so I thought I'd go for a swim. But now,' he added softly, 'I'm back, and you're awake. How very nice.'

'I was looking for my clothes.' She gestured helplessly. 'Do you know where they've gone?'

'Pilar, my housekeeper, has them. They'll be returned to you later, beautifully laundered.' His smile widened. 'And speaking of later…'

He dropped the towel, walked across to her, and picked her up, carrying her back to the bed.

'We can't,' she protested breathlessly as he took her in his arms. 'Do you realise what the time is?'

'Better than you, darling. But no one is looking for us. At least, no one here present,' he added with a touch of wryness. 'Pilar has shepherded her family off to Sunday Mass, and she's left salad and stuff for our lunch—if we ever get round to eating it. She'll be back to cook dinner this evening, but until then we have the house to ourselves.'

He bent over her. 'And I have you,' he whispered.

At the first touch of his mouth on hers she was drawn instantly, eagerly, into the world of the senses she'd discovered last night.

She kissed him back without reserve, her hands stroking their way over his cool skin, marvelling at the strength of bone and muscle, learning him through her fingertips.

Felt her own body respond with joy to his touch, to the caress of his hands and mouth, now suddenly as necessary to her as the air she breathed.

Knew too that she was melting, hot with desire for the final consummation of their lovemaking. The moment when she would belong to him completely.

Diaz took her with immense care, his body gentling its way into hers, his eyes watching her face intently for any hint of discomfort.

But Rhianna was aware of nothing but a sense of completion, as if a missing piece of her life had been found at last.

He said hoarsely, 'Do you know—do you have the least idea what total heaven you are?'

'And I,' she whispered, 'was thinking the same about you.'

As she moved with him, joined to him, she felt like a bird soaring, her only song one sweet, uncontrollable cry of pleasure as her body splintered into the fierce rapture of climax.

Afterwards they lay quietly entwined, exchanging kisses, murmuring nonsense to each other.

'It's just occurred to me,' he said, twining some of her hair round his fingers and breathing its fragrance. 'I'm now potentially the most hated man in Britain.'

'Then it's just as well you're in Spain.' She nestled closer. 'But why?'

'The ultimate fantasy,' he said. 'I'm in bed with Lady Ariadne.'

'No,' she said quickly. 'Don't say that, Diaz. Never say that. She doesn't exist, and you know it.'

'Sweetheart, I was joking.' His tone was remorseful as he tipped up her chin and studied her. 'But I admit I'm curious how you ever got cast in a part like that.'

'Good audition,' she returned frankly. 'Something told me the series was going to be a smash, and I wanted it—even though Ariadne wasn't a leading character originally. But when we went into rehearsal they suddenly realised her potential and began changing the scripts.'

She sighed. 'Now she's seen off two husbands, a lover, and the heir to the estate—the Victorian equivalent of Lucrezia Borgia. Some fantasy.'

'At the same time,' he said, 'stunningly beautiful and incredibly sexy.' He paused. 'In spite of your astonishing state of innocence, my love, you can't tell me that your co-star, however good a friend he may be, wasn't turned on even marginally in his love scenes with you.'

A gurgle of laughter escaped her. 'Rob's an actor,' she said. 'His main concern when we were in bed was ensuring the camera got his best side.'

He stared at her. 'You have to be joking.'

'Not a bit of it,' she said, still giggling. 'Ask the director. Ask anyone. For Rob, love scenes are just work, and he takes that extremely seriously. Besides,' she added more soberly. 'He doesn't play around. He's a one-woman man, which is why I'm sure that he and Daisy will get together again. She's the other half of him.'

There was a silence, then he said quietly, 'Let's hope you're right, and it works out for them.' And began to make love to her again.

And as her body lifted to his touch, the words, *Because it never can for us* seemed to hover unspoken in the ether.

They were still there in the back of her mind, impossible to shake off, when they eventually ate lunch, sitting on a terrace at the rear of the house overlooking the swimming pool, with Rhianna wearing one of his shirts.

'I really wish we'd arrived in daylight,' she said, drawing a deep breath. 'I've only just realised there are mountains.' She shaded her eyes, studying the range of jagged grey peaks towering towards the sky that filled the distance. 'They're spectacular. And is that actually snow I see?'

'It's usually there somewhere on the *cordillera*,' Diaz agreed. 'So are bears, although I admit I've yet to see one.'

She shuddered. 'Just as well, I imagine.' She paused. 'And everything's so *green*. I didn't expect that.'

'We get a fair amount of rain here,' he said, adding laconically, 'Don't confuse Asturias with Andalusia.'

'Here—the mountains. In Cornwall—the sea. You seem to have picked the best of both worlds.' She managed to keep a wistful note out of her voice.

He shrugged. 'I have roots in both. After all, this is where Jorge Diaz was born, even if the original house no longer exists.'

Seen in daylight, the farmhouse itself wasn't particularly beautiful, just a large rambling structure with white walls and a roof of faded terracotta tiles, but it fitted solidly and reassuringly into its landscape.

Like Penvarnon, she thought, it had all the makings of a home.

It suddenly seemed necessary to change the subject.

She waved a fork at the clustering trees beyond the garden's perimeter fence. 'Is that your apple orchard?'

'Part of it.' He offered her some tomato salad.

'My God, she said. 'What happens to all the fruit? I didn't know the Spanish were big on apple pie.'

'These apples make cider,' he explained. 'They drink a great deal of it here in the north. But it's quite mild, unlike scrumpy.'

'And your pool.' She raised an eyebrow. 'After what you said about the house, do you reckon that's a comfort rather than a luxury?'

'I'd say both. You can try it after we've eaten, and give me your opinion.' He smiled at her. 'It's also pretty much a necessity. Asturias has always been a big coal mining area, and most of the rivers are still polluted, so not much swimming there.'

'Can't something be done about that?'

'Yes, but it all takes time.'

My cue, she thought. Aloud, she said lightly, 'Which reminds me—my time here is running out fast. I really need to find out about flights to London.'

'Dressed like that?' His grin teased and warmed at the same time. 'You'll be a sensation.'

She forced a shrug. 'I get my clothes back tonight. I can leave tomorrow.'

There was a brief silence, then he said, 'Of course. I'll see what I can arrange.'

Making her realise just how much she'd hoped he would say, Don't go. Not yet. Stay with me.

Which proves he's far more of a realist than I am, she told herself ironically. A man with roots and his future planned. A future that could never seriously include the girl whose mother wrecked his parents' marriage.

Whereas I—I'm the twenty-first century equivalent of a strolling player, a rogue and a vagabond who performs and moves on.

Had their time together achieved the desired effect? she wondered, pain stabbing at her. Had it cleared her from his mind and appeased his body? When she left, would he finally be rid of her, even if it hadn't happened as he'd expected?

'What are you thinking?' His question cut abruptly across her reverie.

She pulled a rueful face. 'Oh—just that I'm probably going to have some explaining to do when I get back.'

His mouth tightened. 'The questions are already being asked, it seems,' he commented. 'Pilar tells me there were four telephone calls from my aunt yesterday, all bordering on the hysterical.'

Rhianna gasped. 'Even while the wedding was still going on?' She paused. 'Have you called her back?'

'No,' he said. 'She may be my mother's sister, but she has no jurisdiction over my life.'

Rhianna said awkwardly, 'Perhaps she's just being protective—thinking how your—how Mrs Penvarnon would feel if she knew about us.'

'They're hardly close,' he returned drily. 'It suits my aunt to play lady of the manor at Polkernick, while my mother lives in St Jean de Luz, but there are no family visits—not even for this wedding, as you may have noticed.'

'Maybe that's why Mrs Seymour's so upset?' Rhianna suggested. 'Because you weren't there either?'

'I made it totally clear to her that could happen,' he said. His eyes met hers. 'I was there for one reason only, if you remember, and it wasn't to see Carrie throw her life away on that waste of space.'

'And then you found there wasn't really a reason after all.' She tried to smile. 'It's a pity that virgins can't be issued with some kind of barcode. Think of the problems that would have saved you.'

He pushed his chair back with such force that it fell over with a clatter, then came round the table to her, pulling her to her feet.

'Don't say that,' he muttered roughly. 'Don't even think it. Dear God, Rhianna, this may not have been what I intended, but it was what I wanted. You were what I wanted, and I need you still—for whatever time we have left.'

And she went trembling into his arms, closing her mind to everything but the passion of his kiss.

They spent a quiet afternoon by the pool. Rhianna ventured into the water once, but found it cold, much to Diaz's amusement, and retreated back to the padded sun mattress under the huge striped umbrella.

She turned her head, beginning to smile as she watched him emerge from the water.

'For a moment,' she said, 'I thought I was a teenager in the cove at Penvarnon again.'

'My God,' Diaz said, as he towelled down before stretching out with a sigh of pleasure on the adjoining mattress. 'One of my life's most difficult moments, and you still remember it.'

'Of course,' she said. 'You were the first naked man I'd ever seen.'

He grinned at her. 'I thought you didn't look.'

'I certainly tried not to,' she said demurely.

'I see.' He paused. 'And has your attitude undergone any significant change since then?'

She propped herself on one elbow, her eyes openly caressing him, while her free hand began to stray, taking whatever liberties it chose.

'Now,' she said softly, 'now I could look at you for ever.'

'Take all the time you need,' he said lazily, his eyes half closed, magnificently unselfconscious as his body quickened and hardened at her touch, before pulling her to him and making slow, sweet love to her in the drowsy afternoon.

But as they lay together afterwards Rhianna became aware that the breeze had freshened, and shivered suddenly.

Diaz sat up, looking at the sky. 'The weather's changing,' he said. 'See the clouds gathering above the mountains? It's going to rain.' He sighed. 'We'd better go in anyway. I think I heard the car, so Pilar will be back.'

It was, she thought, the end of an idyll...

And the end of everything.

'I hate to think what she'll say if she sees me wearing your shirt.' She kept her tone light.

'Well, she's unlikely to say it to you.' His mouth twisted in amusement. 'I'm the one who gets the full force of her disapproval. She loves me, but she thinks I'm a bad influence on her menfolk.' He added wryly, 'Juan and Enrique are her cousins, and Felipe is her grandson, so she takes their moral welfare very seriously.'

He shook his head. 'She's always said that I'll—' He stopped abruptly.

'That you'll—what?' she queried, then realised. She said hesitantly, 'That you'll break your mother's heart?'

His mouth tightened. 'Something of the sort.' He zipped himself into his shorts, then held the shirt for her to put on.

Pilar was indeed back. They did not see her, but her voice could be heard in the distance, shrilly upbraiding someone.

'Felipe, no doubt,' Diaz muttered as they escaped upstairs. 'He wants to go south to Marbella, to earn lots of money and have fun with foreign girls. Pilar, as you can imagine, is against the idea. War is intermittent, but fierce.'

The first thing Rhianna saw in the bedroom was her clothing, fresh, clean, and laid neatly across the bed.

'Why the hell didn't she put it away in the wardrobe?' Diaz said, frowning.

'Too intimate, perhaps.' She smiled valiantly. 'Also too suggestive of permanence. You'd better reassure her that her fears are unnecessary.'

He turned away. 'I'd better say something, certainly.' He looked down at the dresses on the bed, and picked up the green one she'd worn that first evening on the boat. 'Wear this for me tonight, Rhianna. Please?'

Her heart seemed to twist. 'If—that's what you want.'

'It's what I have to settle for, anyway,' he said, and walked into the bathroom.

Presently she heard the shower running, and realised he had not invited her to join him as he'd done earlier that day, when her attempt to wash his back had turned into something very different. When, with both of them drenched and laughing, she'd found herself lifted on to his loins and brought to a swift and tumultuous climax which had left her clinging to him, her legs too shaky to bear her weight.

She sank down on the edge of the bed, the dress draped across her lap and thought, He's starting to say goodbye.

She dressed with extra care that evening. Diaz had gone by the time she emerged from the bathroom in her turn. Outside, the sky looked like granite, and she could hear the first heavy drops of rain thudding on to the balcony. Everything, she thought, was changing.

She put on her favourite underwear, silk embroidered with little silver roses, and made up her face with a light touch. She brushed her hair to the lustre of satin, then slipped into the green dress, winding the sash tightly round her slender waist.

She even chose the same earrings. Then, after touching scent to her pulse points, she went downstairs.

Diaz was waiting for her in the salon, a long, low-ceilinged room, with creamy walls and the same slightly old-fashioned furnishings that she'd noticed elsewhere, which seemed so much in keeping with the house. The enormous fireplace at one end of the room didn't seem out of place either, she thought, listening to the splash of the rain.

But it was the portrait hanging over the fireplace that brought her to a surprised halt. For an instant she thought she was looking at Moira Seymour, only a frailer, more shadowy version, and then she realised who it must really be.

She said uncertainly, 'Your mother?'

'Yes,' he said. 'Painted not long after I was born. It was meant to hang at Penvarnon, but I had it shipped over here.'

Rhianna looked again. No, she thought. That could never be Moira Seymour. There was a quietness about the seated figure, a softness to the mouth that bore no resemblance to her sister's glossy self-confidence. And Esther Penvarnon looked sad, too. Not at all like someone who'd just given birth to a much wanted child.

She hesitated. 'Will you tell me about her—and your father? After all, it can't make any difference now.'

He stared down into his glass, his brows drawn together. 'I was away at school from the time I was seven,' he said. 'But even before that I knew somehow that they weren't happy. My father was a big man, larger than life and full of energy. He taught me to swim and row a boat, and to bowl at cricket. He made life special, and I pretty much worshipped him. I saw much less of my mother. She suffered constantly from this terrible debilitating virus that left her with hardly the strength to move. I was always being told as a child to be quiet because she was asleep, or keep out of her room because she was resting.'

He added expressionlessly, 'Looking back as an adult, I can see that it probably hadn't been a real marriage for a very long time. There was my mother in a wheelchair, with my father still young, virile, and attractive to women. A recipe for the usual disaster.'

He shook his head. 'I suppose there must always have been other women. Certainly he spent less and less time at Penvarnon, and I began to stay away too, discovering family life in other people's houses.'

She said, 'But your aunt and uncle…?'

'Were there principally for my mother.' His mouth twisted. 'My father thought it would be good for her to have her sister's companionship. The reality, I think, was very different. Eventually someone from the village was employed to care for her—your aunt.'

Rhianna looked at him gravely. 'I would hardly mention Aunt Kezia and caring in the same breath.'

'Yet she was devoted to my mother, apparently,' he said. 'Then, when she was promoted to housekeeper, her place was taken by her younger sister, Grace, who was planning to become a nurse.'

He moved restlessly to the fireplace and stood looking up at the portrait.

'Apparently he fell in love with her at first sight,' he said abruptly. 'So it can't have been easy for him to be married yet not have a wife in any meaningful sense. So maybe there was some excuse for him finding consolation elsewhere.'

He drew a harsh breath. 'But he came back to Penvarnon, Rhianna, and had a blatant affair with a girl almost young enough to be his daughter, totally humiliating and distressing my mother in the cruellest way. Then, when Grace Trewint was dismissed, he followed her to London and lived with her in a Knightsbridge flat he bought for them both. He never came back to Cornwall. We lost him. I—lost him.'

She said, 'But if they loved each other—'

'What kind of love is that?' he returned harshly. 'When so many people get hurt by it? My mother ended up in a nursing home, for God's sake. She was there for almost a year, but gradually she put her life back together. Her health improved, and she even learned to walk again.'

He shook his head. 'But she wouldn't return to Penvarnon—and, with its memories, who could blame her? At first she bought a house in Brittany, then she moved south. But not here. Still not to Penvarnon property.' He paused. 'And she remains—fragile.'

He turned slowly and looked at her, his eyes haunted, anguished. 'Rhianna...'

She went to him, putting her forefinger gently on his lips to silence him. 'You don't have to say anything,' she told him huskily. 'Truly, you don't. Because I—understand.'

We love each other, she thought. But we can never say so. Because he's right. What kind of love deliberately causes more hurt to someone who's suffered enough?

She moved away and sat down. 'Did she never think of divorce?' she asked tentatively.

'That's one of the few things I've felt able to ask her.' Diaz walked to the windows and stood looking out at the rain. 'All she said was, "It wouldn't have been right."'

She said with difficulty, 'She must have loved him very much.' She paused. 'Did you ever see your father again?'

'Yes,' he said. 'When your mother eventually left him he went back to South America, and I spent a lot of time with him there. But he wasn't the same. He looked old and tired, long before his final heart attack. And I blamed her for that too.' He saw her flinch and took a step towards her. 'Darling…'

'It's all right.' She held up a hand, smiling resolutely. 'It's just that I still can't equate the woman I knew with this—this heartless home-wrecker.'

She took a deep breath. 'Which is perhaps the moment to change the subject. Did you manage to find me a flight back to Britain tomorrow?'

'Yes,' he said. 'At five p.m. from Oviedo. The ticket will be at the Transoria desk.'

'Thank you.' She looked down at her glass. 'There's one more thing. Tonight—may I—is it possible for me to sleep in another room?'

Diaz turned back to the window. 'Yes, of course,' he said quietly. 'I should have suggested it myself.' He paused. 'I'll tell Pilar to transfer your things.'

She said, too brightly, 'Another victory for morality. She'll be delighted—especially when she finds I'm leaving tomorrow.'

'Then at least one cloud has a silver lining.' He drained his glass. His smile skimmed her. 'Shall we go into dinner?'

It was a wretched meal, eaten mainly in silence, although the food was superb. There was a delicate almond soup, followed by thin slices of tender beef cooked in wine and green olives, and to finish *crème* Catalan, flavoured with lemon.

She said, 'I didn't think anything could better the food on your boat, but now I'm not so sure.'

His smile was abstracted. 'Hardly surprising. Pilar taught Enrique all he knows.' He rose. 'Would you excuse me for a little while? I have some correspondence I should attend to.'

She said swiftly, 'And, once again, I have to pack.' She paused. 'So, I'll see you tomorrow.'

Her new room was just across the passage from the one she'd shared with Diaz the previous night. Everything had been prepared for her. The shutters had been closed and the lamp lit. The ceiling fan was whirring softly and her nightgown waited on the turned-down bed.

And on the night table was the photograph wallet, which Pilar must have found when she'd been unpacking for her.

Rhianna sat down on the bed and looked at the contents again. The pictures of Ben Penvarnon were the least terrible in the selection, so maybe she should offer them to Diaz, who might like them as a memento of his father.

But she couldn't imagine he'd want the awful ones of Moira Seymour, skulking about in the bushes, she thought critically as she riffled through them. What on earth had Aunt Kezia been thinking of?

I'll sort them out in the morning, she told herself, and began to get ready for bed.

She felt unutterably weary as she lay in the darkness, listening to the splash of the rain, but her mind wouldn't let her rest, imprisoning her on an emotional treadmill of regret and longing.

Images of Diaz smiling into her eyes jostled with the bleakness in his face as he'd talked of his parents' marriage. He'd been a lonely child, she thought, and his initial kindness to her had been prompted when he'd recognised the same sadness in herself.

But now the trap of loneliness was closing round them again, and although she'd tried to armour herself against it by spending tonight apart from him it hadn't worked. She was just wasting precious hours when they could have been creating a last beloved memory together.

Besides, after what they had shared, how could they part in this coldness? It just wasn't possible.

She slipped out of bed and went to the door, quiet as a ghost in her white nightgown.

He might be asleep, she thought as she crossed the passage. Or, worse, he might decide things were better as they were and reject her.

It was a thought that halted her, but even as she hesitated his door opened suddenly, and Diaz confronted her, wearing a black silk robe.

For a moment there was silence, then he said her name very softly, and took her hand.

Colour stormed into her face. 'I couldn't sleep.'

'Neither could I,' he said huskily. 'I was just coming to your room. I thought—I hoped that perhaps you might let me hold you. I wouldn't ask for anything else.'

She said, 'Then I'll simply have to plead for both of us,' and went into his arms.

CHAPTER TWELVE

SHE awoke just before dawn and lay for a moment watching him sleep, before easing herself to the edge of the bed, careful not to disturb him.

He deserved his rest, she thought with tenderness, remembering how he'd exerted all his self-control in order to pull himself back from some edge of desperation when he'd first begun to touch her, and the lingering, exquisite arousal to the aching passion of mutual fulfilment which had followed.

However, Pilar also deserved her illusions, she told herself, rescuing her torn nightdress from the floor and slipping noiselessly back to her room.

So it would be as well to pretend they'd spent the whole night apart.

She dropped the nightgown into her waiting travel bag, and then, her body still glowing with remembered pleasure, slid back into bed.

The rain had stopped, and a grey light was filtering into the room through the shutters. Somewhere in the garden a bird sang.

Another memory, she thought, to be recalled when she was far away, and she turned, burying her face in the pillow.

She hadn't planned on sleeping, but when she eventually stirred the floor was slatted with brilliant sunlight, and a glance at her watch told her it was nearly mid-morning.

She scrambled almost guiltily out of bed and headed for the bathroom. Why had no one woken her? she asked herself, as she stood under the shower. It seemed to her that at some point someone had touched her hair, but that was probably just a dream.

Half an hour later, dressed and with most of her packing done, she ventured downstairs. As she stood hesitantly in the entrance hall, Pilar appeared from the *salon*, according her the beginnings of a smile.

'*Buenos dias, señorita*. You come—eat?'

'Thank you.' Rhianna paused awkwardly. 'I'm sorry I'm so late.'

The housekeeper shrugged. '*No importa*. Señor Diaz say leave to sleep. So I leave.'

A place had been set for her on the rear terrace. Coffee was brought in a tall pot, followed by hot rolls, a dish of honey, and a bowl of fresh fruit. And finally Pilar put a platter in front of her, with a vast omelette filled with smoked bacon, tomatoes, peppers, potatoes and cheese.

'Heavens.' Rhianna surveyed its proportions with faint dismay. 'Just for me?'

'*Por supuesto,*' Pilar returned. 'Of course.'

'The *señor* has had his breakfast?' Rhianna ventured as she poured her coffee.

'Many hours ago.' Pilar gave her an astonished look. 'Then he work on computer, on telephone. Much busy. Now he go to Puerto Caravejo—to boat.'

'Oh.' Rhianna's brow wrinkled as she calculated the distance. 'Do you know how long that will take? It's just that I have to get to the airport…'

'No worry. He say he be here. He will come.' Pilar allowed her another judicious smile and departed.

To her own surprise Rhianna demolished every scrap of the omelette, and ate two rolls with honey after it.

After all, she reasoned, she might not eat again until she was back in England.

She was up in her room when she heard the sound of the car. Her lift to the airport, she told herself. She picked up her bags, took a last look around to make sure she'd forgotten nothing, then started for the stairs.

She would greet him smiling, she told herself. And not a word or a gesture would betray how much their separation would cost her.

As she turned the corner a bright light flashed in front of her, and she halted, blinking. In the same instant she realised that it was not Diaz waiting in the hall below but two men, one of whom was just lowering a camera.

The other was the reporter from the *Duchy Herald*, Jason Tully. 'Hello, Rhianna.' His smile was triumphant. 'I just knew we'd meet up again.' He looked at the luggage she was carrying. 'Going somewhere?'

'Yes, back to England.' She spoke calmly and continued her descent, putting the bags down at the foot of the stairs. But under her surface composure she felt sick, and her heart was going like a trip-hammer.

'But not back to Cornwall, I hope? You're *persona non grata* down there, as I imagine you know.' He paused. 'I suppose you *have* read my exclusive in the *Sunday Echo*? No?' He took a folded newspaper from his pocket and handed it to her. 'Be my guest. And you might want to sit down.'

Something warned her to do as he said, and she seated herself on the bottom step. As she opened the paper, the strapline above the front page leapt out at her.

Castle Pride star's wedding shock: 'He's mine,' says tearful Donna.

Oh, no, she whispered silently. Oh, God, please, no.
The story, with pictures filled the whole of page three.

Wedding guests at a picturesque Cornish church were left stunned yesterday when Donna Winston, rising star of hit TV series *Castle Pride*, halted the ceremony, claiming, 'I'm having the bridegroom's baby!'

Donna, twenty-two, told the shocked congregation that she and Simon Rawlins, scheduled to marry childhood sweetheart Caroline Seymour, had been involved in a passionate three month affair, which had left her pregnant.

Standing at the altar rail, just minutes before the arrival of the bride, Donna turned weeping to the blond, six-foot groom and declared, 'You're my baby's father, Simon. You belong to me, and I won't let you go.'

Ushers hustled the distraught Donna out of the church amid the murmurs of horrified onlookers. Standing in the sunshine, she declared defiantly, 'Simon's been living a lie. But it has to stop. He has responsibilities.'

She also revealed that she met twenty-six-year-old Simon through her former flatmate, Rhianna Carlow, and that many of their passionate love trysts had actually taken place at the *Castle Pride* star's Walburgh Square pad.

'Rhianna knew exactly what was going on,' she said. 'Even though she's supposed to be the bride's lifelong friend. But she must have had a recent attack of guilty conscience, as she's been trying to bully me into having an abortion. I wouldn't do it, because I know Simon loves me, and our baby is part of that love.'

Meanwhile, inside the church, the Vicar of Polkernick, the Rev. Alan Braithwaite, announced that both the ceremony and the lavish reception for two hundred guests would be indefinitely postponed.

As disappointed friends and family left the church, the bridegroom and best man departed by a side door, refusing to comment.

Also unavailable was Rhianna Carlow, who allegedly aided and abetted the secret affair, and whose portrayal of scheming, immoral Lady Ariadne in *Castle Pride* has raised eyebrows all around the world.

According to local reports she has not been seen since she left a prenuptial party hand in hand with glamorous multimillionaire Diaz Penvarnon, whose gracious home, Penvarnon House, was due to host the cancelled reception.

It is believed the couple decided to boycott the wedding for a love tryst of their own aboard the millionaire's luxury yacht, which sailed from Polkernick Harbour on Friday evening for an unknown destination.

Meanwhile the betrayed bride, pretty twenty-three-year-old Caroline Seymour, is being comforted by her family, with callers barred from the Penvarnon mansion.

Rhianna drew a deep breath and looked at Jason Tully. 'Not such an unknown destination after all, it seems.' She tapped the paper with a contemptuous finger. 'Well, you've already done your worst, Mr Tully, and earned yourself a national by-line. So why are you here?'

'To confirm a few things and make some more money.' He looked around. '*Very* cosy. But where's the boyfriend? Still sleeping off the Ariadne effect?' His smile was a lecherous insult. 'Hasn't lasted, though, your grand passion, has it? Maybe it occurred to him that having Grace Trewint's daughter as his mistress was a bit too close to home.

'Oh, yes,' he added softly, as Rhianna gave an involuntary gasp. 'People couldn't wait to fill me in on the old scandal—not when they heard what you'd done to Miss Seymour. Your name's dirt in Polkernick. And lucky me has another exclusive. I gather the wronged wife lives just over the French border,' he went on. 'What will she say, I wonder, when she hears that her son's been following so closely in his father's footsteps? Will she be impressed? I don't think so.'

Rhianna said calmly, 'The most you'll get is "no comment". I can promise you that. Anyway, why involve her when you have me? I'll give you what you want to know.'

She got up, smoothing her dress and smiling. 'As you've guessed, it was just a brief fling.' She slowed her voice to a drawl. 'One of those things that happen when you've both had too much to drink, alas. I threw myself at him, and he caught me. Something that seemed like a good idea at the time, but wasn't. And now it's over, and I'm out of here.' Her smile widened. 'If you're heading for the airport I'd be glad of a lift.'

For a moment Jason Tully looked almost nonplussed. 'You have no plans to meet him again?'

'Absolutely none,' she said. 'We agreed on just one thing—enough is definitely enough.'

'Right,' he said slowly. 'And what are you planning to say to Caroline Seymour next time you see her?'

How was it possible to stand and talk and function with some semblance of normality when you were hurting so much? When all you wanted to do was sink to your knees and howl?

She shrugged. 'I have no idea, but I'm sure I'll think of something.'

'And how do you react to rumours that your *Castle Pride* contract may be cancelled after the next series has been shown?'

She certainly hadn't been expecting that, she thought, flinching inwardly. Who said there was no such thing as bad publicity?

She said lightly, 'Merely that all good things come to an end.'

She was braced for another question, but at that moment Pilar suddenly erupted on to the scene from the back of the house, her voice rising in a crescendo of fierce Spanish as she flourished a threatening broom at the startled Tully and his companion.

'Hey!' he shouted as the bristles grazed his shoulder. He turned on Rhianna. 'You tell her that's assault, and I'll have the law on her.'

'I think she'll tell you this is trespass,' Rhianna returned evenly. 'Also this is her country, and her boss is a respected figure locally, so don't count on the police being on your side. I'd just leave, if I were you.'

She didn't expect her advice to be taken, but with a lot of muttering they went, and she heard the car drive away.

It was only when she felt Pilar's hand on her shoulder, and the older woman's voice urging her to be calm, that she realised she had sunk back on to the bottom stair and was sitting with her face in her hands.

She said shakily, 'Pilar, I have to go now. This minute. I must get back to England. Get an earlier flight if I can. Could Felipe drive me to Oviedo?'

'Felipe is disgrace,' Pilar said icily. 'He let in men—strangers—to the house of Señor Diaz. Take money. Bring dishonour on family.' She paused. 'Better you wait for the *señor*.'

'No!' Rhianna grasped her hand. 'I can't—not after this.' *I can't face him. Not after what's happened—and what I've said.*

She went on, 'Whatever Felipe's done, I really need him to drive the car. Please, Pilar. Tell him to take me to the airport, *por favor*.'

There was a silence, then Pilar nodded reluctantly.

'*Ay de mi*.' She raised clenched fists. 'What I say to the señor when he comes? What I tell him of men in house?'

Rhianna handed her the crumpled newspaper. 'Just give him this,' she said quietly. 'It will explain everything. And now will you get Felipe, please? Because I really have to go.'

'You're not serious.' Daisy stared at Rhianna open-mouthed. 'You're coming out of *Castle Pride* because of this nonsense? Darling, you don't mean it.'

'Yes,' Rhianna said steadily, 'I do. I've realised I simply can't do it any longer.' She pushed the tabloid newspaper she'd brought with her across the kitchen table. 'This decided me.'

She pointed at a large picture of Diaz walking along a street, his face cold and fierce with anger as he realised the presence of the camera, and at the screaming headline which accompanied it: 'He laid Ariadne and lived! Millionaire's drunken sex romp!'

She shook her head. 'Oh, God, how vile and sordid is that? Diaz is the last man in the world to want his private life gloated over in this ghastly way. Especially now that the papers have all picked up the story about my mother and his father being lovers.'

She attempted a smile. 'My attempt at a diversionary tactic has just made things a thousand times worse. I've failed everyone, including myself. But I've been well punished for my failure. Diaz must really hate me after all this.'

Daisy picked up the coffee pot and refilled their cups. 'Well,' she pointed out reasonably, 'as you've sworn you're never going to see him again that hardly matters. Nor are you responsible for something that happened long before you were born.' She paused. 'Besides, *you* didn't drag Diaz Penvarnon on board a yacht and sail off with him into the wide blue yonder. That was all his own idea, and if it's backfired—tough. It's certainly no reason to jeopardise your entire career.'

She gave Rhianna a long look. 'What on earth did your agent say?'

Rhianna bit her lip. 'Plenty.'

'I bet,' said Daisy. 'And the production company probably said even more.'

'I haven't had their reaction yet,' Rhianna returned. 'Although I've reason to believe they won't be too upset. Not that it will make any difference.' She leaned forward. 'Don't you see? In everyone's minds I've turned into Lady Ariadne—this monstrous creature. She's become the reality instead of me. And I can't handle that any more. When I started playing her it all seemed quite harmless, but it isn't any more. And I—I need to get away from it all. To get away from *her*.'

I've also realised I don't want to take off any of my clothes again in front of anyone but the man I love, she thought with sudden anguish.

'Just don't be too hasty.' Daisy put a comforting hand on her arm. 'Because it won't always be like that. This Donna Winston rubbish will soon be forgotten.'

'Not,' Rhianna said bitterly, 'by me. Or by many other people while she's on every daytime TV chat show, banging on about her fight for love and the safety of her unborn child. Making me into the real-life villainess of the piece.'

'Whereas, of course, the actual villain has got off scot-free.' Daisy wrinkled her nose in distaste. 'According to one story I read, he's vanished to South Africa—and good riddance.' She hesitated. 'Have you managed to contact your friend in Cornwall yet?'

'No,' Rhianna admitted dejectedly. 'I've tried phoning the house, but they won't let me speak to her.' She stared into her cup. 'And last time, when her mother answered, she called me a treacherous bitch.'

'And why wouldn't she?' Daisy said robustly. 'You've said yourself she's always hated you. She needs someone to blame, that's all.'

'She and a million others,' Rhianna said unhappily. 'I feel I'm a step away from being stoned in the streets. I came here this morning in a wig and a pair of sunglasses so no one on the Tube would recognise me. And though the Jessops have been wonderful, as always, letting me stay with them while the press are camped out at my flat, it can't be a permanent arrangement.'

She sighed. 'I feel I need to go and hide somewhere that no one will ever find me.'

'As long as you come out of hiding in six months' time,' Daisy said agreeably. 'Because you're going to be wanted as a godmother.'

'A *godmother*?' Rhianna sat up sharply, her own woes temporarily on hold. 'Truly? Oh, Daisy, my love, that's so wonderful.' She hesitated. 'Is that why Rob…?'

'Went into panic mode and ran?' Daisy supplied, brows raised. 'Absolutely. My beloved idiot suddenly saw a future where all the work had dried up and he had a wife and child he couldn't support. He got all the way to his parents in Norfolk, realised he was insane, and came back.'

She began to smile. 'Now he's given up the idea of being theatrical knight and his lady in favour of being a patriarch, with his family and their golden retriever in the garden of their palatial country home.'

There was a silence, then Rhianna collapsed in the first fit of genuine laughter she'd experienced since her return from Spain over a week before. Daisy joined her.

'God bless our boy,' Rhianna managed weakly at last, wiping her eyes. 'Incorrigible, or what?'

She was still smiling to herself as she made her way back to the quiet road where the Jessops lived.

Mrs Jessop met her in the hall, her kind face concerned. 'You've got a visitor, dear. A lady. She's in the front room.'

Carrie, Rhianna thought as she pushed open the door and went in. Oh, please, let it be Carrie.

Instead, she saw a tall woman with silvered blonde hair, dressed in immaculate grey trousers, with a matching silk blouse, and a coral linen jacket hanging from her shoulders.

For the first startled instant, as her visitor turned from the window to face her, Rhianna thought that it was Moira Seymour, and braced herself for the inevitable onslaught. But this woman was smiling at her. Diffidently, perhaps, but quite definitely smiling.

'So.' It was a soft, clear voice. 'Grace's daughter. We meet at last.'

Oh, God, thought Rhianna, panic tightening her throat as she recognised the face from the portrait. It's Diaz's mother.

She said uncertainly, 'Mrs—Penvarnon? I—I wasn't expecting this. What are you doing here—and how did you find me? I don't understand.'

'To be frank, I hoped you'd never be obliged to,' the older woman returned wryly. 'But when Diaz sent me the photographs he'd found in your room and demanded an explanation, I knew I no longer had a choice.'

'The photographs?' Rhianna stared at her. As soon as she'd got back to London she'd realised they'd gone. That they'd somehow been missing from her bedside table when she cleared her room. 'You mean Diaz had them?' She added with constraint, 'But why would he send them to you when they were mainly shots of his father?'

'Mostly,' Esther Penvarnon corrected her quietly. 'But not all. There were—others.'

'Well, yes,' Rhianna agreed, still puzzled. 'There were several of Mrs Seymour, plus a few taken with her husband. But I don't see…'

'No,' the older woman said. 'It wasn't Moira with her husband. Those photographs were of me—with my lover.'

'You?' Rhianna looked at her, stunned. '*You* were having an affair?'

'Yes.' The reply was steady. 'An affair with my brother-in-law, Francis Seymour. He and Moira had come to live at Penvarnon when I'd first become ill, to provide me with company and run things when Ben was away. He used to sit with me in the evenings and read to me, or we'd listen to the radio together. Gradually our relationship—changed.

'It wasn't a trivial thing,' she added with emphasis. 'We were both unhappily married and we fell deeply in love. Although I realise that is no excuse for the damage that was done.'

'But you were in a wheelchair,' Rhianna protested.

'I had been, certainly,' Esther Penvarnon returned. 'But my health had been slowly improving for many months. However,

I chose for my own reasons to maintain the fiction that I was helpless.' She paused. 'May we sit down? It might make what I have to say a little easier for me.'

Rhianna drew a deep breath. 'I think that's a good idea.'

Esther Penvarnon seated herself in the armchair on one side of the fireplace, and Rhianna occupied the opposite one.

'Firstly,' Mrs Penvarnon began, 'my husband did not leave me because of some illicit passion for your mother. Grace Trewint was only ever resident housekeeper at his London flat—and a much needed friend. Ben told me so in a letter he wrote to me not long before his death, and I believe him. He left Cornwall, and the home he loved, because he too had been shown photographs, far more damaging ones than those Diaz saw, proving that I was being unfaithful to him, and he was devastated.

'Your mother wasn't dismissed because of any wrongdoing, either. She'd left of her own accord weeks before, because she suspected the truth and wouldn't lend herself to such gross deception of a good man. And Ben Penvarnon *was* a good man, Miss Carlow. He was also very rich, dynamic, and extremely handsome, and he attracted women like wasps round honey. He was just—not for me.

'I'd always been the quiet one, you see, living in my sister's shadow. So I was flattered—dazzled—when Ben fell in love with me, not her, and I somehow managed to convince myself that I must love him too.' She stared into space, as if she was contemplating an image too terrible to bear. 'However, the realities of married life soon taught me differently. I felt—nothing for him. Eventually I became sick with dread whenever he came near me.'

Rhianna moved restively. 'Mrs Penvarnon, I don't think you should be telling me these things. They can't matter any more.'

'Ah, but they do. Because they're my sole excuse for the continued pretence that I was ill. I was cheating the kind, considerate, generous husband who loved me for a long time before Francis and I became involved. And I think that was what he could not forgive—the lengths I went to in order to avoid being a wife to him.

'Once he'd gone, the three of us that were left went to even greater lengths to make sure the truth didn't get out. Moira was too fond of being lady of the manor to contemplate divorce. And I—I was shattered, and wanted only to get away. So when Kezia Trewint began to spread her tissue of lies we denied nothing.'

'But she took the photographs,' Rhianna said slowly. 'Took them, then showed them to your husband. Why did she turn on him?'

'Because she was in love with him—obsessed by him.' The older woman shrugged wryly. 'She believed, poor creature, that he'd be grateful to her, and much more besides. But he left by himself, and when she learned that Grace was working for him all that hidden passion turned sour, and she deliberately twisted their relationship into dirt.

'And I let her,' she added sombrely. 'Even after Ben's letter I said nothing. I told myself there was nothing to be gained by the truth. That Moira and Francis had patched up their marriage, and by this time even had a child. Best, I told myself, to let sleeping dogs lie. To go along with the myth of the betrayed wife.'

Esther Penvarnon paused. 'But none of us bargained for you—Grace's double—reawakening all the old resentment and all the guilt.' She added quietly, 'And I didn't allow for the possibility, my dear, that my son might love you so much that he would insist the record be set straight and your faith in your mother vindicated at last.

'So I'm here to ask if you can forgive me. If some good can finally come out of the sorrow and bitterness of the past, and there can be healing.'

There was a silence, then Rhianna said slowly, 'Perhaps—if it was just the past. But it isn't.' She lifted her chin. 'I'm grateful that my belief in my mother has been justified, but I can't go any further than that. You see, Mrs Penvarnon, nothing's changed for me. My whole life is a mess. A disaster. I was drawn against my will into a totally unacceptable situation where I was also forced to keep other people's secrets. As a result I've been vilified in the tabloids and on television.'

She got to her feet, her legs shaking under her. 'My career, such as it was, is finished. My attempt to protect the happiness of my best friend has been a disaster. Her life is ruined, and she'll probably never speak to me again. And my relationship with Diaz, which began for all the wrong reasons anyway, has been dragged through the gutter press and distorted beyond recognition. You've seen the papers. How could he ever want to know me again—even if his sense of honour has demanded that the truth must be told?'

She drew a trembling breath. 'I got everything so terribly wrong—even with the best possible motives. All in all, I've caused more trouble than my Aunt Kezia ever dreamed of. Yes, I can forgive what happened in the past, if that's what you want to hear. That's the easy part. After all, the people most affected by it are no longer with us to be hurt any more. But this is the present, and I've had my own conspiracy of silence to contend against, and lost.

'I'm alive, Mrs Penvarnon, but who is there in this entire world who will ever forgive me? And how can I possibly bear it?'

From the doorway, Diaz said gently, 'With me beside you, my dearest love. We'll get through it together.'

Rhianna swung round, staring across the room at him with a kind of anguish. 'How did you know where to find me?'

'I've always known,' he said. 'Did you really think I'd let you leave Penvarnon five years ago without reassuring myself that you were safe and being cared for? When I found the press camped outside your flat, I guessed where you'd be.'

'But you can't stay here. You have to go—go now.' And she turned away, covering her face with trembling fingers.

In the silence that followed she heard the door close, and for a moment she thought he had really left her. Then his hands descended firmly on her shoulders, pulling her round to face him, and she realised that it was Esther Penvarnon who had departed, leaving them alone together.

He said quietly, 'Darling, without you, I'm going nowhere. You're the other half of me, and I refuse to live without you. So get used to the idea.'

'How can I?' She looked up at him with desperation, her clenched fists pushing at his chest. 'If the reporters trace you here, they'll crucify you all over again.'

'For what? Another drink-crazed orgy?' He grinned at her. 'It sounded terrific. I only wish I could remember it. Could you arrange an action replay some time?'

'It's not funny.' Her voice was almost a wail. 'I told that revolting Tully man that we'd just had a brief fling to try and get rid of him. He was threatening to talk to your mother—to tell her about us—and I couldn't let him do that.'

'It would have got him nowhere. She already knew.'

She stared up at him. 'She did? But how?'

'I told her myself, much earlier that same day. Not long after I woke up and found myself in bed alone, and realised I might be doing that for evermore unless I took positive action. I'd spent the better part of my life avoiding my family's no-go areas, but with my entire future happiness in jeopardy it was time to call a halt.

'So I rang my mother, told her we were lovers, and that I intended to bring you down to St Jean de Luz that day on *Windhover* to meet her. I was half expecting tears, accusations and hysterics, but instead there was the oddest silence, before she said very calmly that it might be best, as there were things that must be said, and that she would see us later.

'I went to your room to tell you, but you were deeply asleep and I didn't want to disturb you. However, I saw the photographs beside your bed and decided to have a look at them. And then I was the one to be disturbed,' he added drily. 'All this time I'd just accepted what I'd been told about my parents' marriage. I never questioned it—even when I knew I was falling in love with you. Suddenly my whole perspective underwent a radical change, and I realised what my mother might be waiting to say. So I sent the photographs to her via my computer, and gradually the whole miserable story came out.'

Rhianna shook her head. She said in a low voice, 'It must have cost her a great deal to tell you—and to come here today.'

'She says it's been a relief to speak the truth at last, and not have all that deception hanging over her any longer. She admitted she was always terrified that if I found out I might not be able to forgive her. After all, my father wasn't the only one to be kept at a distance by her supposed ill-health. But I think she's been punished enough.

'So, I told her that I was more concerned with how the whole sorry story had affected you. That I couldn't forget the lonely, unhappy child who'd come to Penvarnon to live under her mother's supposed shadow. Or that, with the exception of Carrie, we'd all treated you pretty badly. And I was one of the worst,' he added sombrely. 'Especially when I realised what I'd begun to feel for you and tried to end it.

'Only I never could, Rhianna. In all those five years I couldn't put you out of my mind, no matter how I tried.' He grimaced. 'And I did try. I didn't want to be torn apart between my need for you and my family's potential outrage. I still believed, you see, that my mother was too emotionally fragile to cope with the notion of my spending my life with you. My aunt Moira hinted that any nervous strain could lead to another breakdown.

'When you'd gone, I tried to tell myself I was suffering from a simple case of sexual frustration. That if I'd taken you to bed I'd have got you out of my system. However, eventually watching you as Lady Ariadne didn't help one bit. And when I saw you again I knew that wanting you physically was only part of what I felt for you. That somehow you were still the scared, isolated girl I yearned to love and protect for ever.

'And I was going to tell you so—only finding you with Rawlins stopped me in my tracks. The night I spent outside your flat, imagining you with him, was the lowest point in my whole existence. Yet even then I still ached for you. So when I learned you were defying me and coming to the wedding I made my plans accordingly. I tried to tell myself that I was taking you away for Carrie's sake, but that was sheer hypocrisy.

'Only then I found myself in bed—not with the practised seductress I'd expected, but the innocent girl I'd longed for and believed I'd lost for ever.' He gave an unsteady laugh. 'Dear God, I didn't know whether to turn a cartwheel or slash my wrists. What I had to do—and quickly—was rethink all my assumptions and win you round to the idea of being my wife. And no past scandals could be allowed to interfere.'

'But we still have the present ones to contend with,' Rhianna reminded him unhappily. 'And it's Carrie we have to think of now.' She bent her head. 'I was trying to protect her, and I've made everything a thousand times worse. And Donna Winston keeps adding fuel to the flames every day.'

'Well, the inventive Miss Winston's fire is about to go out,' Diaz said with distaste. 'It seems, my darling, that Rawlins wasn't the only one to give her money for the proposed termination. A guy she'd been seeing in Ipswich also paid for the same privilege. He kept quiet when the story first broke, because he was trying to salvage his marriage, but his wife has now left him so he's spilled the beans. The news will be in all the tabloids tomorrow. I think a lot of attitudes will change very quickly.'

'But that won't make things any better for Carrie.' Rhianna tried unavailingly to release herself from his arms. 'And how can I let myself begin to think of being with you when she's so wretched—and hating me? The Seymours are your family, Diaz, and we can't pretend they don't matter. That they won't do everything they can to stop us being together. You didn't hear how Carrie's mother spoke to me.'

'I can imagine,' Diaz said calmly. 'But I'd be surprised if that had much to do with her daughter's feelings. She's far more concerned about the past resurfacing so inconveniently, and losing her status as mistress of Penvarnon House to you, sweetheart. It seems she married Uncle Francis mainly so that she could stay in Cornwall and live at Penvarnon, maybe making my father realise, at the same time, that he'd chosen the wrong sister.'

His mouth twisted. 'But she was the mistaken one. He let her run the house for him, but that was all. Sadly for him, he loved my mother, and I believe he did so until the day he died.'

He paused. 'And don't worry too much about Carrie, my darling. Yes, she's still shocked and hurt, but she's had a lucky escape, and I think she's starting to recognise it. We went for a long walk together a couple of days ago, and she admitted she'd sensed there was something wrong in the weeks before the wedding. That Simon had changed so much there seemed to be little left of the boy she'd fallen in love with all those years ago. She'd even begun to wonder if she was doing the right thing, although she managed to convince herself it was bridal nerves.

'And she certainly doesn't hate you, whatever her mother may imply. She says she knew that you'd been wary of Simon for years, and avoided him as much as possible. So you'd hardly have played Cupid between him and your flatmate.'

He bent his head and kissed her gently on the lips. 'She'll be fine, my love. Just give her time.'

She moved closer, resting her cheek against his chest, her whole body warming to his nearness. 'But it may not be the same between us,' she said, with a touch of sadness.

''No,' he said softly. 'But how could it be, darling? Because you're going to be my wife, and that's bound to change things anyway.'

He picked her up in his arms and carried her over to the armchair, settling her on his knee. 'Now, can we just think about ourselves for one minute?' He reached into an inside pocket and produced a flat leather case. 'I have a present for you.'

From their satin bed, Tamsin Penvarnon's turquoises gleamed up at her.

'Even if I can persuade you to marry me incredibly quickly,' he went on, as Rhianna gasped, 'these have to be part of the ceremony.' He kissed her again, slowly and sensuously. 'And we'll take them on honeymoon with us,' he whispered. 'I want to see you wearing them and nothing else on our wedding night.'

There would still be gossip, and even more newspaper headlines before they'd be allowed to live in peace with each other. But with Diaz beside her Rhianna knew beyond all doubt that she could face anything life brought her. That their love would guard them always.

'It will be my pleasure,' she answered softly, and slid her arms round his neck to draw him down to her in promise and trust.

Darkly handsome—proud and arrogant
The perfect Sicilian husbands!

RAFFAELE: TAMING HIS TEMPESTUOUS VIRGIN
by
Sandra Marton

The patriarch of a powerful Sicilian dynasty,
Cesare Orsini, has fallen ill, and he wants atonement
before he dies. One by one he sends for his sons—
he has a mission for each to help him clear his
conscience. But the tasks they undertake will
change their lives for ever!

Book #2869
Available November 2009

Pick up the next installment from Sandra Marton

DANTE: CLAIMING HIS SECRET LOVE-CHILD
December 2009

www.eHarlequin.com

HPI2869

HARLEQUIN *Presents*

TWO CROWNS, TWO ISLANDS, ONE LEGACY

A royal family torn apart by pride and its lust for power, reunited by purity and passion

THE ROYAL HOUSE
of
KAREDES

Look for the next passionate adventure in
The Royal House of Karedes:

THE GREEK BILLIONAIRE'S INNOCENT PRINCESS
by Chantelle Shaw, November 2009

THE FUTURE KING'S LOVE-CHILD
by Melanie Milburne, December 2009

RUTHLESS BOSS, ROYAL MISTRESS
by Natalie Anderson, January 2010

THE DESERT KING'S HOUSEKEEPER BRIDE
by Carol Marinelli, February 2010

HP12867

She's his mistress on demand—but when he wants her body and soul, he will be demanding a whole lot more! Dare we say it…even marriage!

PLAYBOY BOSS, LIVE-IN MISTRESS
by *Kelly Hunter*

Playboy Alexander always gets what he wants… and he wants his personal assistant Sienna as his mistress! Forced into close confinement, Sienna realizes Alex isn't a man to take no for an answer.…

Book #2873

Available November 2009

Look for more of these hot stories throughout the year from Harlequin Presents!

www.eHarlequin.com

HP12873

EXTRA

SNOW, SATIN AND SEDUCTION

Unwrapped by the Billionaire!

It's nearly Christmas and four billionaires are looking
for the perfect gift to unwrap—a virgin perhaps,
or a convenient wife?

One thing's for sure, when the snow is falling outside,
these billionaires will be keeping warm inside,
between their satin sheets.

**Collect all of these wonderful festive titles
in November from the Presents EXTRA line!**

The Millionaire's Christmas Wife #77
by HELEN BROOKS

The Christmas Love-Child #78
by JENNIE LUCAS

Royal Baby, Forbidden Marriage #79
by KATE HEWITT

Bedded at the
Billionaire's Convenience #80
by CATHY WILLIAMS

www.eHarlequin.com   HPE1109

You're invited to join our Tell Harlequin Reader Panel!

By joining our new reader panel you will:

- Receive Harlequin® books—they are FREE and yours to keep with no obligation to purchase anything!
- Participate in fun online surveys
- Exchange opinions and ideas with women just like you
- Have a say in our new book ideas and help us publish the best in women's fiction

In addition, you will have a chance to win great prizes and receive special gifts! See Web site for details. Some conditions apply. Space is limited.

To join, visit us at
www.TellHarlequin.com.

THBPA0108

REQUEST YOUR FREE BOOKS!

2 FREE NOVELS PLUS 2 FREE GIFTS!

PASSION GUARANTEED SEDUCTION

YES! Please send me 2 FREE Harlequin Presents® novels and my 2 FREE gifts (gifts are worth about $10). After receiving them, if I don't wish to receive any more books, I can return the shipping statement marked "cancel". If I don't cancel, I will receive 6 brand-new novels every month and be billed just $4.05 per book in the U.S. or $4.74 per book in Canada. That's a savings of close to 15% off the cover price! It's quite a bargain! Shipping and handling is just 50¢ per book*. I understand that accepting the 2 free books and gifts places me under no obligation to buy anything. I can always return a shipment and cancel at any time. Even if I never buy another book, the two free books and gifts are mine to keep forever.

106 HDN EYRQ 306 HDN EYR2

Name	(PLEASE PRINT)	
Address		Apt. #
City	State/Prov.	Zip/Postal Code

Signature (if under 18, a parent or guardian must sign)

Mail to the **Harlequin Reader Service:**
IN U.S.A.: P.O. Box 1867, Buffalo, NY 14240-1867
IN CANADA: P.O. Box 609, Fort Erie, Ontario L2A 5X3

Not valid to current subscribers of Harlequin Presents books.

Are you a current subscriber of Harlequin Presents books and want to receive the larger-print edition? Call 1-800-873-8635 today!

* Terms and prices subject to change without notice. Prices do not include applicable taxes. Sales tax applicable in N.Y. Canadian residents will be charged applicable provincial taxes and GST. Offer not valid in Quebec. This offer is limited to one order per household. All orders subject to approval. Credit or debit balances in a customer's account(s) may be offset by any other outstanding balance owed by or to the customer. Please allow 4 to 6 weeks for delivery. Offer available while quantities last.

Your Privacy: Harlequin Books is committed to protecting your privacy. Our Privacy Policy is available online at www.eHarlequin.com or upon request from the Reader Service. From time to time we make our lists of customers available to reputable third parties who may have a product or service of interest to you. If you would prefer we not share your name and address, please check here. ☐

HP09R

**Stay up-to-date
on all your romance
reading news!**

The Harlequin
Inside Romance
newsletter is a **FREE**
quarterly newsletter
highlighting
our upcoming
series releases
and promotions!

Go to
eHarlequin.com/InsideRomance
or e-mail us at
InsideRomance@Harlequin.com
to sign up to receive
your **FREE** newsletter today!

You can also subscribe by writing to us at: HARLEQUIN BOOKS
Attention: Customer Service Department
P.O. Box 9057, Buffalo, NY 14269-9057

Please allow 4-6 weeks for delivery of the first issue by mail.

IRNBPAQ209

I ♥ HARLEQUIN Presents~

BROUGHT TO YOU BY FANS OF
HARLEQUIN PRESENTS.

We are its editors and authors
and biggest fans—and we'd
love to hear from YOU!

Subscribe today to our online blog at
www.iheartpresents.com

HPBLOG